# DAUGHTER *of* WINTER

# DAUGHTER *of* WINTER

## Pat Lowery Collins

**CANDLEWICK PRESS**

Copyright © 2010 by Pat Lowery Collins

First edition 2010

Library of Congress Cataloging-in-Publication Data
Collins, Pat Lowery.
Daughter of winter / Pat Lowery Collins. — 1st ed.
p. cm.
Summary: In the mid-nineteenth-century shipbuilding town of Essex, Massachusetts, twelve-year-old
Addie learns a startling secret about her past when she escapes servitude by running away to live in the
snowy woods and meets an elderly Wampanoag woman.
ISBN 978-0-7636-4500-7
[1. Identity — Fiction. 2. Wampanoag Indians — Fiction.
3. Indians of North America — Massachusetts — Fiction.] I. Title.
PZ7.C69675Fe 2010
[Fic] — dc22    2009049099

10 11 12 13 14 15 16 BVG 10 9 8 7 6 5 4 3 2 1

Printed in Berryville, VA, U.S.A.

This book was typeset in Rialto Piccolo Roman.

Candlewick Press
99 Dover Street
Somerville, Massachusetts 02144

visit us at www.candlewick.com

In fond memory of my grandparents,
Harriet and Mathias Meyer

YESTERDAY I washed their bodies
as I've seen the women do,

dressed them in their best,
and laid them in a crypt of snow

until such time as I can steal
a pine box from the pile

behind the hearse house, drag it
back here on my sled, and wait

until the earth thaws.
It's such a distance from the town,

you can't hear hammering
in the Yards or cries of "Frame up"

that disturb our teacher
and ricochet through headstones

where we play.
It's icy quiet here today,

without my brother's prattle
and the rattling sounds my mother

made before she died.
I hold Matilda's purr

against my chest. I talk
out loud to calm myself.

And while there's light,
I write to Papa out at sea

to tell him Mama's better since the flux
and Jack is learning how to count.

•     •     •

# *one*

ADDIE DIDN'T STOKE THE FIRE in the stove but let the embers turn to ash. She didn't light a single candle when the blackness settled over everything the way it always did so far away from town. She only half remembered fixing her eyes on the windowpane above the sleeping loft, where stars pricked with fevered sparks, and how she'd crooned to herself, in a voice so shrill and unfamiliar, so like an animal's cry, she hardly recognized it as her own. The two quilts she'd pulled around herself couldn't make her warm or stop the shaking, and she sank into the blackness at last, not stirring until Demetry gave his morning crow. There was such cheer in it that she ran screaming from her bed and barefoot through the yard, flapping her arms at the rooster, and stopping only when she felt the biting cold creep under her nightgown and saw that more snow had fallen in the night.

It startled her to see how the snow crypt, in morning light, appeared to be just a little hill that Jack could play on. For a moment she didn't think of him and Mama so cold and still inside it. For just a moment. And then the whole unimaginable day ahead, the terrible weeks just past, cast such a heavy pall over the present that she seemed unable to move. Why hadn't she been able to save them? Because Addie had always been the one to bring down Jack's fevers in the past, Papa had once called her a healer and claimed she was descended from a healing tradition. If it was true, why had she been powerless in the face of this loathsome illness that had claimed so many?

A low painful mooing from the barn reminded her she hadn't milked Fleur for two days. With no calf to feed, the poor heifer would be engorged with milk. Only the cow's urgent need propelled Addie back into the house for shoes, a coat, and a clean pail. Even when Mama and Jack had been most sick, she hadn't neglected the cow, whose sweet milk had at times been all the food that Jack would take. Warm from the animal, it had helped to keep up her strength as well. She couldn't let the cow get sick.

As she pulled on the teats with slow, even strokes, she allowed her mind to go where it continued to be drawn — to the hardest part, when closing first Mama's eyes, then Jack's, had shut the window on their souls. Now she thought how there had really been no spirit left in their empty blue stare, eyes so alike in life, identical in death. This closing was a thing she'd also seen the women do, and although she probably couldn't explain it, she now knew the reason.

But she hadn't expected how small and light Jack's body had become. She was accustomed to the weight of him in games of piggyback and when she'd swung him around in circles; in death, his slack form within her arms was inert as a bag of flour. Mama seemed to have shrunk and was curled into a fetal pose, which Addie had to straighten some before she stiffened, in preparation for the box she'd need to fit in. Addie had carried her fragile form, wrapped in a clean sheet, with a strength she hadn't known she could summon. That she had obeyed Mama's wishes not to allow a stranger's hand upon either of them was very little consolation.

She felt as if Mama and Jack were just waiting now — waiting for a proper place to rest, away from all the elements and threats of wild animals, such as that fox that sauntered by the henhouse at summer's end. Mama'd shot at it to scare it off. She'd only just learned to use a rifle, and Addie'd been amazed to see her, such a small, frail woman, wield it in this way, as if she'd always handled firearms. Addie thought how she couldn't have known then how soon she'd need this same skill and wished her mother had taught it to her. There were many things she now wished that she knew how to do — things she either hadn't had the patience to learn or that Mama didn't know herself or hadn't had the will or patience to teach. Even before Mama took sick, their nearest neighbor, Mrs. Tower, would sometimes come by to help her sew a dress or kill and clean a hen. And though she'd learned to weave and embroider while still a girl, she rarely encouraged Addie's awkward attempts at either.

After milking Fleur and feeding the chickens, the hours of the day had hovered about her, colossal and blank, like tremendously large saucers that needed to be filled. But with what? She seemed to have lost the key to ordinary days.

"I do have a plan," Addie said into the empty house. "I do. I know what has to come next."

Hearing her own unwavering voice both surprised and reassured her. She went over in her mind again how tomorrow she would take her sled into town before the sun was up. She'd travel an ancient Agawam Indian trail that snaked along the fields where there'd most likely be deep morning mist, thick as sea smoke when the river froze, to shield her from the eyes of anyone awake. And soon she'd have to find how to get her letter to Father on his way to the California goldfields on the schooner *Metropolis*.

If he knew the truth, she was certain he'd either find some way to leave this expedition that meant the world to him or else she'd be sent to live with any stranger who'd agree to take her in. Addie'd seen it happen to another girl at school. A smart girl, too, she hardly came to lessons anymore, too busy tending someone else's house and family. Another child had been moved to a neighboring town to help care for children not much younger than himself. Recently, the ailing Mrs. Spinny, who lived just across the field, had been looking for a hired girl, and she'd relish getting one for free. Addie felt downright revulsion at the thought of tending that lady of many complaints and her bossy husband, passed out most evenings from the effects of his own corn liquor. Hadn't Mama, time and again, warned about the interference of strangers until Addie had an outright fear of even those who happened by just to be neighborly?

"Go up into the loft, Addie," Mama would say before she'd open the door even a crack. Or, "Run out the back and tend to the chickens."

Mama had even resisted sending Addie to school. It was Mrs. Tower, her mother's only real friend, who had finally convinced her to.

"Emmaline," Addie'd heard one day from the stoop where she was sitting as the two women conversed inside the house.

"You've got to let the child get book learning. She's such a clever little girl. You can teach her a few"—she cleared her throat—"of the homely arts, but they won't be enough for her to get on in life."

Mama's low protests had been almost indistinct. But Mrs. Tower had continued. "She'll be all right. You'll see. Children are so accepting."

Afterward, Addie had asked her mother what the word *accepting* meant. Mama chided her for listening in, but then had said, "It's just one of those big words Mrs. Tower likes to bandy about. You know how she is." But she did, reluctantly, begin to send Addie to school.

On her way there or on Addie's infrequent forays into town with Pa, the sideways glances of most townsfolk had made her feel—how could she describe it?—a little different from the people hereabouts. She was never quite sure why. Living so far from the clusters of small houses that ringed the center, the only time she saw other children besides the sprawling nearby family of Towers was at school or on her rare visits to church with Pa. He would attend from time to time, but Mama liked to say that she "communed with the Divine" in private. Addie didn't know just when she did that or what divinity she conjured up. Papa's seemed to be a distant God who sat up in the clouds; Mama's was apparently too deep inside her to glimpse.

Still, Addie was convinced there was a force at work within her life much bigger than she was, so powerful that it had been able to turn her whole world around in just a space of weeks. She had no image of this force, no catechism lessons to draw upon like the Tower children, who could earn a holy card for answering such a question as "Who made you?"

Papa liked to say how God didn't cause bad things to happen. How He just allowed them. She wondered what kind of God could have allowed such a terrible thing to happen to her just when her father had left on such a distant journey that he couldn't be reached.

"Adelaide," she remembered him saying on the very day he'd made the decision to buy passage on the *Metropolis*, joining a small group of gold-rush speculators on a copper-fastened vessel fitted for a two-year cruise. She'd long been aware that he liked to use her full name when he was feeling important. He then explained how they'd be leaving on November 15 in this year of 1849. "It's an investment. If we hit it rich, I can buy your mother the life she wants — a big house, a buggy. One day I may even be able to commission the building of a schooner of my own and take command of it myself."

In the wooded area they had been passing through, red and gold leaves swirled from the trees, and evergreens poked through the changing landscape like winter emissaries. Addie and her father were walking across the fields together and had climbed to the top of a hill that offered the best view of Ipswich Bay. He rubbed the stubble on his chin, and she thought how it was growing in darker than the hair on his head and would soon be a full beard that she wouldn't see for a long time. His eyes had looked away to the horizon and fastened there. His mouth had grown as soft as his words. "It's an absolute dream come true."

She remembered feeling a creeping fear rather than the excitement he seemed to expect and wondering how they would manage on their small homestead without his help. Her mother — never very strong since Jack had been born, and given to long silences and sick headaches — had grown up in the big house of a merchant in the city of Salem. If coaxed, she'd sometimes tell of the life she'd led before her own father's "reversal of fortune," how she'd had a governess, learned French, and filled a hope chest with linens and laces and fine china, some of which were now, unused and dusty, on the shelves that Papa'd built for their small house in Essex. As Addie tried to think of some argument to keep him from leaving, she looked down at her own hands, which were small replicas of her father's large capable ones. She thought of how she had his dark hair and eyes as well, which often caused second looks from strangers when she was out with her fair-haired mother and brother. At twelve years old, she could already tell that she was going to be tall like him, too.

"What about your job in the yards?" Addie asked. "What about the two dollars a day you've been promised?" He'd been so proud of his recent raise in pay.

"I'm speaking of a possible fortune, Addie. A fortune in gold." His eyes held a peculiar glint that made her uneasy. He caught strands of her glossy windblown hair in his hand and held them away from her face. "If I do fail—and I won't—there'll always be jobs for dubbers and caulkers like me in a shipbuilding town like Essex. We've nothing to lose."

Today Jack's toys, Mama's loom, Papa's books—books by men such as Bronson Alcott and Nathaniel Hawthorne and Henry David Thoreau, who preached about survival in the woods and the simple life—stood out like intruders that had no real reason to be there. Papa had been reading the slim Alcott book to Addie, *Conversations with Children on the Gospels*, in the days before he went away, and there was a ribbon marking his stopping place. Now, just before dusk, the weak winter light threw important shadows of even the smallest objects across one wall of the largest room. Addie moved into the only corner where they couldn't find her and where she could, even for a little while, be hidden away from all the things she feared were bound to come.

She kept the fire going in the stove this second night and made a bed on the hard floor in front of it, holding Matilda close. Tears soaked her pillow between snatches of sleep. Every small sound that had once been woven through the warp of her nights punctured the dark like a sharp stick. A passel of dry leaves blown against the door was the scraping of a ghost's bony hand; the scavenging raccoon outside the privy mimicked the shuffle of a stranger's feet through soft snow.

While the waning moon seemed caught in the branches of an aspen, and before a pink dawn began to show through the transom, she was awake and dressed, fastening the buttons of her knee-high winter boots and pulling Papa's old woolen watch cap over her long dark hair to both hide it and keep her warm. She put on the trousers she wore for mucking the horse stall and hoped she'd be taken for a boy if anyone saw her about the fields so early. So tired she wasn't sure how she was going to complete the task she'd set, she wished she'd searched for the sled yesterday. It had been such a long time since she or Jack had used it, and she wasted precious minutes before she finally discovered it hanging from the wall of the shed. As she took down the cumbersome thing, she thought how she'd have to move quickly through neighboring fields before anyone was awake and could notice her, before, as Mama liked to say, prying eyes could turn into wagging tongues.

Even without a passenger, the sled was heavier than she remembered. Always before, she had pulled Jack, as he laughed and urged her to go faster, or they'd both lain on their stomachs so she could help him steer down a slope. Now the weight of her heart and the high snowdrifts made it difficult going even on flat land. Just as she'd hoped, the mist was thick—thick enough at times to obscure certain landmarks she was counting on. As she pulled her scarf over her nose and mouth, she looked up to see the edge of Henry Dunbar's paddock and realized with a start that she must have passed by Mr. Crocker's stile already. She'd have to watch closely so as not to miss the turn she'd need to take across Bullock's field. If she failed to see that, it would be miles before there'd be another place where she could cut over the road.

Though the mist was clearing in places, it settled, abundant and white, into the shallow valleys and ditches along the way. She was focused on one such cloudy mass straight ahead when it began to rise into the air, geyser-like, to become a gauzy figure with arms outstretched, long flowing hair, and an aura of golden light. For minutes it seemed as if the snow had been lit on fire. Addie jolted backward into the snow, dropped the sled's rope, and put a hand over her mouth to stifle her cry. Her disbelieving eyes could not close, however, until she'd made sense of this apparition, which was surely from another world. When it seemed to take on features—eyes and a mouth, large ears—and when the cavernous mouth began to speak, she fully expected some message from her mother on the other side.

"Feather and shell," Addie thought she heard the voice say. Its words were laden with years and intoned like a dirge. "I have kept your feather and shell," it seemed she heard then, though this second time the words were more fuzzy and indistinct and the figure was already moving away from her. A vision, she reasoned, would simply fade from view. This was something solidly human and alive.

Not until it turned and shuffled off across the field did Addie pick herself up from the snow. Her eyes followed the strange being as it grew smaller and smaller and until it ultimately disappeared.

*two*

IT WAS STILL BARELY LIGHT when she reached the undertaker's home, but Addie knew she'd have to work fast before
the man or his wife was up. His house and the town hearse
house were right next to the cemetery that surrounded the
school, and from the window near her desk, Addie had noticed
how the man usually emerged late in the morning and then
only on the day of a funeral or to put a coffin out back or take
one inside. Though it was still foggy, she could make out three
new coffins near the stairs, only one of which was large enough
for Mama and Jack together. Her baby brother had been part
of her mother before birth, she reasoned, and belonged with
her in death.

The box was actually not as heavy as she'd feared it would
be, but it was such an awkward shape — wide near the top and

narrow at the bottom — that she had a hard time balancing it on the sled. The scraping noise of wood against wood was so loud to her own ears, she felt sure someone in the mortuary must have heard it. She held her breath as a candle was lit in one room and a face appeared at a window. She bent down under the sill and didn't move for what seemed an eternity. There was a murmur of voices within, the back door squeaked open, and a large shiny nose protruded into the cold, lit by a weak shaft of early morning sun.

After a minute or two, the door slammed shut, but Addie kept her frozen pose. Not until the candle was finally snuffed out and she heard creaking bedsprings, followed soon by muted snoring, did she decide that it was safe to leave. Her feet seemed too stiff, however, to begin the long trek back. She had to set each boot down with all her will and might, and remind herself of her purpose here and how she needed to do this for Mama and Jack. And Papa. Of course for Papa. As the blood rushed into her toes, so painfully it made her groan, she dragged the sled and its cargo through the snow, under fences where it would fit and around others, and, at last, across the open meadow far away from town.

By now the sun was fully up and anyone could have seen her caravan of one sloshing through the fields. Maybe they would be curious; maybe they would think she was on some boy's errand of no importance. She would have to hope that she was either unobserved or that she presented too insignificant a sight to be paid any mind.

She had already fed and milked Fleur and secured the empty coffin inside the shed — angled against an inside wall in order for the door to shut — when she saw John Tower loping up the road, his book strap flapping around his knees. From a distance, his mop of cinnamon hair looked like a tight-fitting cap, and as he drew closer, she could see how a ragged shock of it was sticking out from his forehead like a visor. He had the same Christmas grin he broadcasted every day of the year, especially in her direction, but today she had such a difficult time smiling back and pretending that nothing was wrong that her cheeks ached. It was Monday of another week, and she should have remembered he'd be stopping for her, but she hadn't thought past her urgent early morning errand.

"You can't go to school dressed like that," he declared when he drew closer to her. As always, his clear but speckled blue eyes flashed as if it were not an ordinary day and as if he'd come to take her on an adventure. If only he knew how un-ordinary this day and the days preceding it really were.

She released her hair from Papa's cap and stuttered a response. "I — I — I'm not going today. Mama, you know. And Jack. They still — they still need me."

"You'll get way behind," John said, scowling too deeply, she felt, and with too much concern. He shook his head, crossed his feet, and leaned on the open gate. "You've already missed the boresome studies on the China trade and a heap of fractions that are really hard. I'll tote your books back on my way home tonight so you don't come a cropper."

She tried to gather her thoughts as quickly as she could. Usually when he was bossy like this, she'd sass him right back. But she knew he was right and that if she didn't return to school soon, people would begin to wonder. And each time John came by the house to bring her lessons, there'd be more chance for him to discover the true state of things.

"It's all right," she said finally. "There's no need, 'cause I'll be in school soon enough. Mama's bound to get her strength back real quick now." This lie didn't come easily, but she was surprised that it came at all. She'd known it would be harder lying to John than to anyone else.

"But there is something you can do for me." She pulled the letter from her pocket. It was addressed to Emerson Hayden, Esquire. "You can give this to Mrs. Hardy in the shipping office. She'll know how to get it to my father on the *Metropolis*."

John worked at the yard of Epes Story after school and knew most everyone important.

"Well, of course I can," said John in a teasing way, "that is if I don't lose it first, or Bullock's dog don't tear it out of my hands when I wave it at his teeth."

"It's important, John. No fooling." Tears gave her eyes a dark shimmer and spilled down her cheeks.

"Hey, Addie. I was only funnin' with you. You know." He put a hand out as if to brush her cheek, then let it fall limply at his side.

She wiped her face with one finger, leaving a dirty streak from nose to ear, and didn't look up.

"Something the matter?" he asked.

She couldn't let him think that. With a weak little groan, she said, "You know how it is when your mama's sick, how you have to do all the chores." His mother had the flux earlier in the year and was almost fully recovered.

"Yeah," he said. "I was sure glad when my ma could get back on her feet and I didn't have to watch those porch babies Tyler and Sarah Jane and keep track of the other kids night and day. She says she's still not feeling up to snuff, leastwise she would've helped your mama more. Sometimes it's no good being the oldest. I'll bet Jack's a handful."

Jack had never been that, she thought. She wished with all her heart that he could be.

"And I almost forgot," John added. "My ma wanted me to ask if she can come by as soon as she's not feelin' so weak. She'd like to bring her pork pie if you're up to some."

"We're fine," said Addie, so abruptly she feared sounding ungrateful and turning John suspicious. She quickly added, "Mama's got no appetite as yet. Please thank your mother. Tell her we appreciate the thought." The last part was what Mama had always said to anyone she felt might want to meddle.

When Addie realized he wasn't going to argue with her, her breathing came more easily. The muscles in her face relaxed.

"All right," he said as he took the letter and put it with his books. Then he added, "Don't worry so much. I'll take care of this first thing."

But he looked at her a little too long, a little too quizzically.

She managed a smile, waved him along, then watched as he galloped down the path like a fine colt and across the same fields she had just traveled through. She thought how if he'd come by only minutes before, he would have caught her on her grim mission.

She resisted entering the empty house, but after feeding the few chickens and the mare, she needed to get out of the cold and was suddenly hungry. The soft jingle of the clamshell wind chime plucked the chord of her unbearable loneliness and made her reluctant to go back into what had been a sick-room for so many weeks. When she stepped onto the granite stoop, her toe hit something and she quickly pulled back. Bending down, she noticed a tiny basket filled with a kind of seed she didn't recognize. Had her mother put these out for the birds before she fell ill, the seeds would have been long gone by now. And the basket. She'd never seen one like it before, so tightly woven that the sides were smooth. The compact shape of it begged to be cradled in one hand. With the other, she pushed open the door.

Matilda jumped down from the dry sink and startled Addie into nearly dropping what she held. The cat rushed past her and in minutes had darted out the door, around the henhouse, and disappeared into the fields. She hadn't eaten the food left for her, and Addie wondered if her pet was also feeling sad and confused, if she had an animal's way of knowing what had happened here.

Addie's fingers traced the faint geometric pattern on the basket before she put it on a shelf. It had no relevance to what she needed to do. As she looked around the room, she saw the space more clearly than she had in days. But things were in such disorder that she didn't know where to begin—a pile of soiled bedding in the corner; a long-un-emptied chamber pot; blankets that smelled of camphor, mustard plaster, and sickness; a cracked pitcher in a pool of dirty water; open and broken bottles of medicine; a heap of dirty dishes and spoiled food. She leaned one hand against a smudged pane and stared at her dark fingers outlined in frost. Papa once said her fingers were long enough to play the piano. Addie'd seen one in the church once, and she'd heard about the small piano — a spinet, Mama had called it — that used to be in the parlor in Salem.

A cloud of sleep enveloped Addie as she was thinking about Mama's hands, how they were as small as a child's. It was so insistent that she curled up on the floor in her outer garments without a thought to whether it was morning or night. When she awoke, there was a fire in the grate and Matilda was snuggled against her. But the hopeless confusion of the room was apparent even in the faint flickers of light, and she was confounded as to how a fire that had grown cold could ignite all on its own. She got up to search the darkened room for a candle, and as she passed a closed window, her eyes traveled to the blackness outside it, blackness that was suddenly penetrated by the shadowy specter of a wizened face framed in wild white hair.

*three*

THE TERRIFYING SIGHT had been so brief that Addie wondered afterward if she had been fully awake or still dreaming. Trembling and exhausted, she bolted the door, climbed to the loft and her own disheveled bed, and slept there until morning.

She was awakened by bright sunlight and intense pangs of hunger. She hadn't taken the time to eat for days and was aware at last of just how weak and ravenous she truly was. The ready solution was to milk Fleur first thing and drink almost the entire pail of warm creamy liquid with two hard biscuits she'd found in a back cupboard. Afterward, she built a small fire in the woodstove and fried the few eggs she'd been able to collect from the henhouse.

Finally feeling strong enough to do something about the shambles around her, she repeated her father's favorite adage, "First things first," to the empty room and began a desultory and childish attempt to set things in order.

The first thing, she supposed, had to be to get rid of any human and medicinal waste and throw out the spoiled food. Then, having no way to quickly heat the well water properly, she filled the washtub with frigid buckets of it and scrubbed the bedding on a washboard with lye soap her mother had purchased from Mrs. Tower in the fall. Addie's knuckles were red and raw when she finally was ready to hang everything from the line Papa had once strung from loft to chimney peg. The increased dampness in the room made it all the more chilly, so she brought in enough wood to rekindle the stove, grateful that Papa had stacked at least a cord of it against the house before he went away. It didn't escape her notice that so far all of the things that were sustaining her had been provided by others. But she wasn't ready to think about a time when she'd need to provide for herself.

The high mournful howl of a coyote made her think of the next, the most awful chore she had before her. Without delay, the bodies of Mama and Jack had to be secured within the coffin to protect them from wild animals. The thought of revisiting the problem of their temporary burial brought another flood of tears and a great resistance to disturb their present resting place. For untold minutes she felt completely unable to go ahead with what she knew she must. In the past, she'd succeeded in avoiding all kinds of unpleasant duties by dissolving in tears. But such behavior obviously wasn't going to work in this case and probably never would again. In her mind's eye, she saw her father bringing her close to comfort and reassure her; in her head, she heard her mother's no-nonsense voice saying, "There now, Addie. Don't carry on so."

But she hesitated to make a move until she could no longer deny that there would not be anyone to see her tears and take pity on her, no one to help her with anything at all.

"No one," she said, speaking aloud once more in order to hear words in the room, even if they came from her own mouth. "There's no one but you and me," she told Matilda as the cat stretched her calico fur from head to paws. But then she thought of the animals—Demetry, Fleur, Little Star, and the chickens—and didn't feel quite so alone or even oppressed by the care she knew they'd continue to require.

Still buying time before attempting the abhorrent task before her and unable to control her whimpering, she spread sand on the floor and swept it clean, then opened the windows to let in the sea air. Even at this distance from the ocean, you could smell the salt in it, and she breathed deeply to calm herself. When she shut the windows again, there was a pleasant odor to the room that she eventually traced to the little basket of seeds. The aroma was fragrant and exhilarating and helped her forget the noxious smells that had filled the little house for weeks.

Just before dusk, she steeled herself. There was still light enough, the little hill of snow was beginning to melt, and she couldn't let another night pass without doing more to protect the remains of her mother and brother. The sky had darkened during the afternoon and was now briefly lit by the red rays of a setting sun. Approaching the shed, she knew she'd need to work quickly and was all set to open the door and retrieve the coffin when she looked to her left and saw the box on the ground up near some trees, as far back from the road as was possible.

She ran to the snow mound and began to dig with bare hands, but soon realized how little snow remained and that it covered nothing or no one. Frantic at discovering such emptiness, she no longer possessed normal caution or fear. She hurried to the pine box to pry up the cover and stepped back, a hand to her quivering lips, eyes unblinking and wide. Inside it, Mama seemed to be asleep and little Jack was resting in her arms. The skin of each had the blue transparency of a frozen lake, but for one long moment she felt certain that if she spoke their names, she could easily wake them up. The scene was, in fact, so peaceful and loving that she almost couldn't bear to leave it, and she couldn't let her voice disturb it. Sweet-smelling pine boughs served as both cushion and adornment, and the fragrance of those same unfamiliar seeds rose into the air just as Addie slowly, very slowly, closed the lid.

Before dark she fastened it securely with a hammer and nails and gathered enough additional pine boughs to cover it completely. All the while, the mystery of who could have assisted her in this way haunted her. She was disturbed as well that in spite of her mother's admonitions and all Addie's care, strange hands had indeed ministered to her kin. That someone did know of her predicament was certain. The same person must also know of Addie's lie and that she was living alone with it. Was there a connection to the face at the window and the apparition in the field? Were they one and the same? So far, all the ministrations had been for good. Was it possible that this being, this person, might eventually mean Addie some kind of harm? There was no one to ask, no one to run to. She quietly bedded the animals for the night, went inside the house, and closed it up tight, and she kept her eyes from straying to any of the windows by sheer dint of panic and will.

# four

IT WAS TIME. Addie knew it was time, but her reluctance to return to the life she knew so well, the school she'd attended since she was six, was so great she could barely bring herself to get dressed. She washed in a basin of ice water, pulled a flannel petticoat over her drawers, and slipped a rumpled pinafore over her head. Unable to braid her hair without her mother's help, she tied it back with a frayed ribbon and hoped it wouldn't escape too soon in wisps and straggles. Mama would probably be ashamed of how unkempt she looked. All her life Addie had wanted to be fair and small and fragile like her mother, to be like the true lady that her mother had exemplified. It pained Addie to remember the many times Mama had put her fingers to her throat and given those quick gasps that meant that Addie should try to be less clumsy.

She made a breakfast of another egg, some dried apples, and more milk, but she could think of nothing for her lunch pail. Sometimes if a child forgot her noon meal, Miss Fitzgibbon would provide something. Addie'd have to devise another solution tomorrow, but being forgetful would probably work for today.

Up early enough for the milking and to feed the animals, Addie started over the fields long before John Tower was apt to come by. It was a good four or five miles to town, depending on your route, and Addie took the one with the fewest fences to climb. She didn't want to arrive with a torn stocking or ripped bloomer and be any more disheveled than when she'd started out.

The school was locked when she arrived, but the gate to the cemetery was open, and she wandered in among the headstones to wait. Deciphering the inscriptions was a kind of hobby for all the children who could read. There were so many Choates and Burnhams and Storys and Lows, it sometimes seemed as if these faceless dead people were old acquaintances, and Addie longed for the day when her mother and brother could rest peacefully beside them.

The postmistress, Mrs. Hardy, en route to her office near the yard of Oliver Burnham, caught sight of Addie and waved.

"I know your mother's a very private person, but I've been meaning to come by," she called.

"Mama's not up to visitors just yet," said Addie, trying out a little speech she'd rehearsed in her head. "I'll let you know."

Addie was pretty sure no one had an inkling how long this latest illness was contagious for, because women who might have assisted her mother in the past had been slow to offer help or were down with the disease themselves. She was relieved to discover that her little speech had worked just fine, for Mrs. Hardy smiled and nodded and kept walking.

When Mr. Macklin's milk wagon clattered by on its way to the barn, Addie knew it must be close to the hour for school to begin. She was pleased to find that just before it was out of sight, Miss Fitzgibbon arrived, her coat collar pulled up to the edges of her hat against the wind.

"Addie," she cried when she saw her there. "How good to have you back. How's the family?"

"Fine," Addie replied. "Getting better every day."

Miss Fitzgibbon put her key in the lock, and the door swung inward. "I'm so glad to hear it. Been waiting here long?"

"Not long, ma'am. I wanted to be early."

"That's a fine attitude, dear. And, of course, you've missed a good deal. It's never too soon to start catching up."

"Yes, ma'am."

Addie followed her teacher into the largest downstairs room and went right to her desk, where she carefully picked up her slate and gently touched her few books as if they were alive. It was cold as the outdoors, and Miss Fitzgibbon kept her gloves on to put kindling in the stove and light the fire. When she pulled off her hat, her hair glowed red as oak leaves in autumn. Her freckled cheeks were rosy with cold.

"Might leave your coat on awhile more, dear," she said. Then she added, "Here," as she handed Addie a pile of hand-painted charts. Each one was almost identical to the next but different in small ways. THE CHINA TRADE was printed in large letters on one chart and smaller ones on another. Some of the silkworms in the margins looked like squiggles and some like sticks. The Chinese people pictured had eyes like slits, and there were images of badly drawn ships traveling back and forth upon a bright blue ocean, their cargo listed at the bottom of the page in tiny letters. " 'Twas myself made these."

"They're . . . nice . . . real nice," said Addie. Young Miss Fitzgibbon had replaced crabby old Mrs. Petrie just a year ago, and Addie found it curious that she still needed so much reassurance. She had a soft lilting way of speaking. A brogue, Papa called it. Addie had never heard anyone speak this way before. It was lovely and warm.

"There's one for each of the older children. Do you fancy you can remember who sits where?"

At home Addie would have been able to picture every child in their proper place, but faced with all these empty desks, she paused, suddenly uncertain.

"It's all right," said Miss Fitzgibbon. "Sure and it's been such a while, after all." She reached for the stack and took great pains to deliver them herself. She handed Addie a fistful of sharpened pencils that were meant for each member of the class.

As Addie passed back and forth to the desks by the windows, she caught sight of John Tower opening the gate for Fanny Bright. Clive Ogilvy was right behind. Knowing her classmates were close to entering this very room, she stiffened, overcome by the thought that she'd soon be as exposed to their eyes as a naked tree with a message carved into its bark. Would she be able to keep the lie out of her words and face? Would they ask questions she couldn't answer?

Cold winter light rushed into the room as the door burst open and the children entered, the smaller ones clutching Addie around the knees. It was a welcome greeting, and she was grateful for any commotion that shielded her from addressing her chums, which excluded Clive. For reasons she didn't fully understand, that square-headed, pimply-faced boy had long ago set himself up as her archenemy, calling her an Injun one day, a numskull the next. Neither made any sense, for her skin, though not as pale as her mother's, was not dark like any Indians she'd ever seen, and as she was always at the top of her class, she was clearly no numskull. Still, she was resigned to being especially wary of him, just as she had been of Mrs. Petrie, who'd always acted as if Addie had offended her in some unknowable way.

When Addie's back was turned, the Perkins twins crept up on either side of her and surprised her with a kiss on each cheek.

"You wanna get sick?" asked Clive, and he took out a filthy handkerchief and covered his nose and mouth. "My ma says you can't be too careful."

"Addie's family's on the mend now," Miss Fitzgibbon told him. "And Addie seems just fine to me."

"My ma says we don't know much about this flux, that it's a killer of the weak and the young."

"There've been a few deaths, it's true," replied Miss Fitzgibbon, clasping one hand with another and pressing them against her trim waist. She was barely twenty, and Addie had observed that she found it difficult to take charge and lost patience with Clive on a regular basis. "But that's true with any epidemic. And I told you, Addie's family's better now. So take that silly rag from your face, Clive, and go sit in your assigned seat."

John, as always, was glad to see Addie but vexed that she'd left for school before him.

"It isn't a race, John," she said. "I just wanted to get here early on my first day back, and you like to . . . well . . . you sometimes like to lope."

"Lope," he repeated. "And you have a way to fly here, I reckon."

Fanny Bright giggled, and John sank into the desk beside her that had always been Addie's seat.

Annoyed that he'd made such a change, Addie decided to keep her complaint to herself. Unfortunately, the desk that John had formerly occupied was directly in front of Clive. She'd been seated there for just a minute or two when she felt a hard tug on her hair ribbon, and her heavy hair suddenly tumbled around her face. So this was the way it was going to be!

While he was still leaning toward her, she quickly turned, gathered a chest full of air, and breathed it directly into his prissy, self-satisfied expression.

"You — you're trying to kill me!" he sputtered as he jumped from his desk and ran choking to the back of the room. From the far reaches of the corner, he whined, "And I was already puny feelin'."

Miss Fitzgibbon turned to Addie with a stern sidewise glance. "That was a rude thing to do, young lady." Then she looked Clive full in the face and said, "Return to your desk right this minute." She brandished a sheaf of papers at him like a weapon. When he didn't mind, she raised her slightly crossed eyes to the ceiling until the whites showed, and she snapped her lips in exasperation. "Why, you're as fit as a fiddle."

"No, I ain't," declared Clive, and he pulled on his coat and cap. "And I'm goin' all the way back home and tell my ma just what Addie done. Ma'll take a conniption fit for dang sure."

"Quit your jawing," said John Tower, "and sit back down. Addie didn't hurt you none."

But Clive was already on his way out the door, and Addie was settling into John's former desk and copying the sums Miss Fitzgibbon had put on the blackboard. So those numbers with lines between them were fractions. She didn't know yet how to add them up, but she knew there must be some formula to it. The quiet assurance of numbers, the way you could rely on them — these ideas soothed her. And they stilled the turmoil inside her that she feared others could sense. These fractions. They couldn't be as hard as John said. After what she'd had to do in the days just past, she couldn't imagine that anything would ever seem hard to her again.

*five*

ADDIE STAYED AFTER SCHOOL. Her excuse was that she wanted to help Miss Fitzgibbon, but the real reasons were a reluctance to return to that sad, empty house and the need to discourage John from walking with her there. He seemed surprised and a little offended as he waited by the step. When she told him, "You go on, John. I think I'll stay awhile," he hesitated as if to argue, but then Fanny burst from behind her and took his elbow. "You can walk me home, John Tower," she said. She glanced over at Addie, who was still standing in the doorway, and giggled.

"Go right ahead," said Addie. As if they needed her permission. She was glad of an excuse not to answer any of the questions she was certain would occur to John on a long walk. Always exhaustingly curious, he was bound to pick up on how things were not quite right. She was irritated, nonetheless, at the way Fanny clung to his arm and at the fact that he didn't discourage such fawning. Addie hated the changes that came over some of the older boys, how they'd suddenly get all nervous and cow-eyed around the girls. But she never thought to see John acting that way. He'd been her close pal for such a long time — had taught her a million things like how to make a frog gig and catch thumpers, had shown her the best way to curry Little Star. Maybe he would even help her now if she told him the truth of things, but she couldn't take the chance that he might let something slip and alert the very people she was determined to dupe.

"Ah. You still here?" asked Miss Fitzgibbon when she turned away from the blackboard and saw Addie.

Addie took the damp rag out of her teacher's hand and began to wipe the chalk dust away. "I'll do that," she said.

"It really isn't necessary, dear. You have such a long walk ahead of you, after all, and I room just down the street with Mrs. Packer." Addie noticed how she grimaced a little when she said the name of the crabby older lady, and she wondered if it was hard for her teacher to live so far away from her home in New Hampshire, from the brothers and sisters she sometimes mentioned.

"It's . . . to thank you for the meal," said Addie as she picked up the erasers to clap them outside. The sandwich of bread and honey and the hunk of Mrs. Packer's cheese had been unbelievably welcome at lunchtime.

Miss Fitzgibbon took the erasers from her, held her by the shoulders, and led her toward the door. "You'll get home much too late and give your mother cause to worry," she said. The tips of her even teeth showed through her smile as she gently wrapped Addie's scarf around her neck and helped her into her coat. This small caring gesture brought such tears to Addie's eyes that she bent down as if to fasten her boots more securely.

Once outside, she headed in the opposite direction from home and hoped Miss Fitzgibbon wasn't watching. She wasn't going far, just down the hill to the shipping office. Addie knocked timidly on the door before a voice invited her in. Mrs. Hardy was at her desk near the large map with pins in places where many of the Essex-built schooners and brigantines were headed or had already arrived.

"Hadn't expected you yet, child," said the lady. "The Metropolis has not had time to round the Strait of Magellan. Look," she said, pointing to the tip of a continent Addie recognized as South America. "That's where your papa's bound soon. There's some time before they make the turn and start up the other side for California. Rumor has it the entire trip will take some six months' time."

Six months. Papa had said the trip would take quite a while, but Addie hadn't known it would take nearly that long. Would there be any gold left by the time he got there? She got close enough to the map to see the details, the rivers and mountains on the land, the imaginary sea serpents decorating the large expanses of blue water. A schooner would be just a speck upon anything so immense.

"When will he get my letter?" asked Addie. "The one John Tower brought by?"

"Letter? What letter?"

"He brought it yesterday. He told me not to worry. He said he'd bring it right to you."

"Oh, dear. I don't recall. In fact, I haven't seen that boy for days. Epes Story was asking for him only this morning. They've begun to steam the garboards on that new vessel, and he needs his help after school."

The warmth left Addie's face and hands, and she felt as cold as if she'd been standing in the wind. "You didn't get the letter?" she asked, her lips trembling enough to make the words waver.

Mrs. Hardy began furiously riffling through the papers on her desk as if Addie's sudden ashen appearance had propelled her into action. "It's possible, you know, entirely possible, that the boy left it somewhere here when I was out."

Her frantic hands were waving right and left and spraying papers everywhere. "So like him, don't you know."

When Addie stooped to pick some papers off the floor, she recognized her own handwriting and let out a cry of relief.

"Here," she said, holding up the letter she had so painstakingly penned and assembled. "Here it is. It isn't lost. He did deliver it."

"Well, fancy how he dropped it off like that without a word and gave us such a scare. I'll tell that boy a thing or two."

"It's all right, Mrs. Hardy. He did his best, I'm sure. And we've found it, after all."

"Yes, we've done that, but with pure dumb luck, it seems to me." She took the letter from the girl's hand and scrutinized it. "I'll get this over to Gloucester just as soon as Ebenezer comes by tomorrow in the Chebacco boat for the mail basket."

"Oh, thank you," said Addie, and she repeated it over and over.

"But it still will take some time before it reaches your father. There's quite a bit of happenstance involved."

"I understand," she said, even though she actually had no idea what steps were needed in order to send anything so far away over land and sea. She had no choice, however, but to put her hopes in a process that seemed only a little better than a game of chance. Yet other pupils at school wrote to their fathers at sea, and they even managed to hear back once in a while.

"And do you also understand that it's gonna be forty cents to post this?" said Mrs. Hardy.

Addie had brought only half that, thinking it would be more than enough. She fumbled with the coins as Mrs. Hardy began an unbelievable tale of how the letter would be sent by train to New York City and placed on the steamer *Falcon* on its way to the Atlantic coast of Panama.

"From there it'll travel by mule and canoe through actual rain forests. Imagine that! And on to the Pacific coast, where it'll be put on another steamer to San Francisco."

"How do you know all this?"

"Well, it's my job to know, and that's the reason it's so expensive to send a letter in the first place."

Addie sighed. "It sounds like it would take a miracle for a letter to ever reach the person it was meant for." *And like an awful price to pay.* As she reached for the letter and slipped it into her pocket, she thought about the small amount of cash her father'd left behind. "I'll need another twenty cents," she told Mrs. Hardy. And then she thought, *What if I don't send the letter at all?* Either way, Papa would continue to think that things at home were fine. That forty cents wouldn't change a thing, because the lie she'd written down wasn't just something on a page. It was a lie that she'd begun to live.

Outside the shipping office, she stood for a while to gaze down the river at all the activity in the yards spread out one after the other for as far as the bridge and beyond. Epes Story and Adam Boyd had yards above the bridge and below Andrew Story's, and the Burnham brothers had theirs near the middle of the causeway below John James. She couldn't keep the location of the many other yards straight, though Papa had pointed them all out to her, and he had worked at most of them. Positioned as they were along the water's edge, they were a string of busy and noisy worlds with vessels at their center in all stages of completion. Here and there, smoke from the steam boxes drifted into the sky like Indian signals.

When the river swelled with the tide, there would be a launching in one yard at the same time as a keel was being laid in another, or staging might be built for an assembled hull at Burnhams' while frames were being oiled or keels red-leaded at Epes Story's. Frequently cries of "Frame up!" could be heard all along Chebacco River, and this often brought men from one yard to another. It was an exciting place for a man or boy, and she could see why her father and John

Tower were both drawn to it. Just viewing the loud and persistent commotion as she did from this distance stirred her blood and made her feel a part of a wider and more exciting universe.

The children had all scattered and Miss Fitzgibbon had left for the night by the time Addie passed the school again to head home. The sky was as gray as a wolf's coat but striped with sunlight, and she hoped to be at her own door before nightfall. She picked up a branch to trail in the snow and thought how so far everything had gone as planned. It was clear that Miss Fitzgibbon was completely fooled. She regretted the need to deceive John but could see no other way. When Papa was back and she could tell both him and her best friend the truth of things, she was certain they'd understand. But now she realized that Papa wasn't going to be back as soon as she had thought. A year or more was a long time to keep her secret.

With no one to talk to, she found herself counting off landmarks and struggling with an unfamiliar ache that etched her bones. The closer she got to the house, the heavier her feet felt, and she entered the yard with a reluctance that made it hard to move the last short stretch to the doorway. She slumped down on the stoop for some time, dreading to go inside, but then Matilda ran from the barn and curled around Addie's ankles, brushing them in a serpentine dance. As Addie stood up to push open the door, the cat scooted past her, and they entered the lifeless rooms together. It was so quiet and dark inside. Even the large clock over the stairway was completely still, the hands set stiffly at twelve and four, its comforting tick and tock and chime utterly silenced.

# *six*

ADDIE HAD WATCHED HER FATHER wind the large clock every Sunday, had noticed how he took it down from the wall and held it in one arm as if it were a small child to be fussed over. There were so many dials and mechanisms, however, that she hadn't paid any real attention to how he set the hands and wound it up again. Even if she had, there was no way of knowing today's exact time. Of course she could tell by the light and the feel of the advancing hours if it was morning or afternoon or evening, but since she couldn't wind the clock up, how would she know exactly when to start out for school? Among all her other problems, it was a small one, but it nagged her.

A whinny from Little Star made Addie think how the horse hadn't been run for a while. Days actually. Papa always exercised her in the mornings, and Addie had taken her for short runs while Mama and Jack were sick. But today she'd only had time before school to feed and water her, then attend to Fleur and put scratch and scraps out for the chickens. She'd seen, however, how Little Star was developing a thick coat as the winter days grew colder. She remembered how Papa had shod her for running in the snow.

Thinking that she must be feeling lonely and abandoned with Papa gone and Addie away for an entire day, she pulled on her coat and mittens again and went to the barn, where she saddled the mare with a blanket and put the bit in her mouth. First she let her nuzzle both hands — one of which contained salt, the other sugar — while the horse snorted her pleasure.

As she led her out into the night, light from a dim quarter moon burnished her coat and laid a faint silver path across the snow. Using a box for a mount, she straddled her with ease, gave a soft kick with her heels, and held tight to the reins as the snowy fields began to move under the agile horse like clouds. Addie had the sudden sensation of flying through space without stars, her hair fanning behind her like her own dark mane. The shadows of trees were subdued in weak moonlight as she dashed along the rim of woods but kept to open places. Back and forth she raced the young mare, soaring over low hills and through fields that would in summer be high with a neighbor's corn.

In the distance she could see the glow of the kerosene lamp she'd put in the window. It promised an anchor that she wasn't yet ready to reach for. Darkness was everywhere, but she'd always felt it held fewer secrets or threats than the day. Even the wind seemed to speed her passage through the calm of this beautiful after-hours world. The strength of this release, the momentary shedding of fear and cares that had weighed so heavily upon her, confounded her. For as long as she could, she clung tenaciously to this immeasurable feeling of freedom and wasn't prepared to let it go until she felt warm perspiration leaching through Little Star's coat. She would have to get her back to the barn soon and rub her down. The temperature was dropping, and she would need to go into that house again and allow the walls to close around her like the home it used to be before her father had left.

Ready to enter it with a bravery she hadn't possessed in daylight, she reached for the doorknob, and her fingers snagged on something fastened to it. In the feeble lantern light, she identified a clutch of English ivy, boxwood, and juniper tied with a piece of straw. Had John been by? Who else would have left such a bouquet? She took it off cautiously before entering the house, then went directly to the shelves holding her mother's china and took down a delicate hand-painted vase, something she would never have dared do if Mama were still alive. It couldn't matter to her mother now, she reasoned. There was no longer any voice to say, "Those are my things, Addie. None of those beautiful pieces were ever meant for you." Not even Mama used the special dishes. So Addie hadn't minded her words at first. But when Jack was born, her mother made a point to tell Addie that the china was meant for Jack's wife, whomever that might be. And though Papa had heard what she said, he didn't contradict her or add anything himself. She remembered thinking that maybe it was a rule or something. Maybe boys inherited their mother's treasures and girls did not. But she still felt a deep hurt, as if this exclusion were caused by something she had done.

But now that there would never be a "Jack's wife," Addie thought the vase a much better container for her winter greenery than a butter crock or jelly jar, and there wasn't anyone to stop her from using it. Always so eager to please her mother in the past, it was a distinctly odd feeling to have no one to please but herself. There was peace in the graceful arrangement of greenery, a small nugget of what she had found in her race through the night, and she felt that the mysterious person who had left it for her could not have had any ill intent. Still, she locked the door and closed the curtains.

An airy, cramping sensation in her gut made her conscious of her own hunger, and she suddenly remembered the winter stores she hadn't needed to touch while Mama was so ill. When she climbed into the cellar and began to explore, she found what Papa had told her would be there — a barrel of root vegetables, one of potatoes, some salted cod, packets of dried soups, pickles, peach preserves, and applesauce, most of which he had prepared and stashed away in preparation for his absence. He was very proud of the soups, whose stock had been reduced such that Mama could just add water and create a meal. Mama's contribution to the mix had come from her cherished spice cabinet that contained such things as dried rosemary and thyme, which she doled out sparingly. Growing and collecting spices was one of the womanly arts of which Mama had approved, the others being embroidery and, of course, the fine craft of weaving.

Addie was filled with a rush of longing for the sounds that had accompanied her evenings not so long ago — the squeak of the treadle up and down, the whisk of the shuttle through the threads of the loom. Sometimes the sounds served as a lullaby for Jack as she held her sleepy little brother in her lap.

She sorted aimlessly through the larder to try to dispel the sharp pains of loss, then picked up a soup packet marked VEGETABLE and a jar of peach preserves. She mounted the cellar stairs and put water on to boil in the kettle on the woodstove, not wanting to carry coal to the new iron range that neither she nor Mama had really known how to use. She found a bag of flour in a kitchen cupboard and determined to make bread with it one day when she could figure out how.

The congealed soup was gluey but changed into a thick fragrant mixture under streams of boiling water. It warmed her winter bones and tasted like summer. It made her miss the days spent with her father in the garden — long sunny days when they'd planted seeds, tended the new green shoots, and then harvested their small crops.

She meant to put her head down on the table for just an instant, but when she opened her eyes, sunlight was filtering through the curtains and bringing objects in the room back to life. One arm was asleep and her back was stiff. How could she have slept so long in such an uncomfortable position? What time was it? Would she be late for school? What concerned her most, however, was that it was clearly morning and Demetry hadn't crowed.

# seven

SHE FOUND HIM RIGHT NEXT TO THE BARN, his golden talons sticking into the air, his blank eyes fixed, the iridescent feathers spread like a quilt beneath his inert form. A trickle of blood escaped his beak and pooled beneath the regal cock's comb on his rigid head. As best she could see, his neck hadn't been wrung; he hadn't been shot at or bashed with a shovel. It looked for all the world like death from natural causes, but he had been so sprightly only yesterday that she couldn't help speculating on the intervention of something human or ghoulish. Quickly the fearlessness of the night before, the tranquil feelings, began to desert her.

On her way to school, Addie brooded on how, though it had been Mama's idea to get the chickens in the first place,

Addie'd been the one to care for them. She thought back to that happier time when Papa had built the roosts and winter pen, and to when the chicks, including Demetry, had arrived to take up residence there. He'd been a strutting little thing even then, and she would miss the cheerful noise of him. There was definitely more urgency now to the need for a timepiece of some kind.

The younger children were already at recess skipping pebbles at the headstones or playing tag, and the older ones were working on their maps of China when Addie slipped quietly into the schoolroom and behind her desk. Clive was absent just as she'd expected and hoped, but so was John, which concerned Addie until she recalled that he'd probably received Mrs. Hardy's message and was working in the yards. He played truant a lot when there was a push on to get a vessel planked and ready for caulking. As strong as some of the older men, some days he even ran off to the yards just to help lift frames in place. His father, who worked for Willard Burnham, was skilled at beating out the futtocks with a broadax. He was teaching John this method of cutting out these large curved pieces of wood for the hull, and many expected him to follow in his pa's footsteps. Since everyone knew that such a worker would be in great demand, Miss Fitzgibbon rarely insisted John attend lessons that might interfere with his future livelihood.

Fanny leaned over and told her what she already knew. "John's working again."

"Why so tardy, Adelaide?" asked Miss Fitzgibbon when she looked up from the board. "Mother and child not worse, I hope."

"No," said Addie. Then quietly, "Forgot to wind the clock." No need to tell that she didn't know how.

Miss Fitzgibbon's genial expression collapsed a little. "I'm that surprised at such an excuse from you," she said. "Please make sure to . . . a . . . wind your clock tonight and be here on time. You've already missed a good deal."

"And put out the cat," Fanny whispered.

The twins snorted, and Fanny gave Addie a nudge. Addie had a sudden desire to tell that her rooster had died but decided no one would think that particularly important.

"Back to work, class," said Miss Fitzgibbon. She pushed some stray hairs into her bun and patted her bouncy side curls. "You can copy the names of cities right onto your slates and find them later on your maps. Mariah, please call the young ones back inside and help them with their outer clothing."

That had always been Addie's job, and she felt as if she had angered the kind Miss Fitzgibbon and was being punished for something she couldn't help. She clenched her fists under the desk and squeezed her eyes tight to hold back the tears, which lately seemed always ready to spill over.

Her lunch pail held a hard-boiled egg, the last of the stale crackers, an entire jar of applesauce, and a container of fresh milk. At mealtime, as casually as if she did it every day, she climbed up on the dunce stool at the back of the room where the others couldn't spy on her pail's contents and make comments. The children laughed to see her there, and she played as if it were just a prank.

Smoke backed up into the close space when Miss Fitzgibbon fueled the stove with damp wood, and as the afternoon lessons droned on, Addie's eyes smarted and became heavy. When she caught herself nodding more than once, she struggled to stay awake. No wonder John preferred to be out in the fresh, clean winter air. If John had shipbuilding in his blood, what was in her blood that made her so restless, that caused her to ride into the wind at night and feel the turning of the world?

On her way home from school that afternoon, she crossed the road at Bullock's field and came across another figure slowly ambling along the fence. Though the person's back was turned, he or she seemed to be waiting for Addie to catch up. This had the perverse effect of making her slow her footsteps and approach the walker with caution. She would have had to crawl, however, in order not to come apace before too long.

When close behind, Addie saw from the leather breeches and wildly colored skirt tucked up into her beaded belt that it was the old Wampanoag woman who often appeared throughout the town and its surroundings and always traveled alone. Papa had been known to purchase her very large squash and sweet corn on occasion, and once last summer she'd come to the door with a basket of clams and Mama had complained that Addie's father had paid too dear a price for them. Afterward, there'd been agreement, however, that there was nothing like the feast of steamed littlenecks and melted butter that Papa had prepared. Today the woman had a heavy cloak over her head and shoulders, and she held it close to her with both hands.

"Good day," said Addie as they passed. She knew no Wampanoag words but suspected that the woman would recognize a common greeting.

Swiftly, the old lady thrust her long fingers toward the girl and gripped her free hand. Addie jumped at the sudden rough hold. It scratched her skin and felt more like the claw of an animal than a human touch. At first she twisted away, but as soon as Addie stopped moving, the Indian woman released her and spoke.

"It has been two moons since your father left you to seek gold. One flood tide."

How did she know this? Why was she saying it?

As yet the woman had not looked into Addie's face, but when she did, Addie couldn't contain her horror. She stepped back and raised the hand that had just been freed to her mouth. The face. This woman's face. She had never paid attention to it before in chance encounters. Now so near that she could smell tart apple on breath steaming from the cold, the features sprang at her—the black eyes, the thin lips, a string of small moles beneath the hairline, the wizened cheeks—and she saw again that same face as it had appeared in her window only nights before, framed by hair as white as the snow on the ground.

Perhaps sensing her unease, the woman said, "Please don't be afraid." She said it twice, in a calm voice that seemed meant to reassure Addie.

What the woman said next, however, was not something she had ever heard before, from her father or anyone else.

"My name is Mary Goodrich, but you should call me Nokummus. As a child, I was known as Oota Dabun, which means "Day Star." Then she added, "You"—and she pointed to Addie and then to herself—"we . . . are people of the morning light."

The name Day Star puzzled Addie. She had never seen a star in daylight, and it seemed such a fanciful name for someone as old as this woman who lived alone in what could often be a cruel landscape. And yet she must have been a little girl once

54

who brightened the day. But *people of the morning light*. What did those words mean exactly, and why had this old person included her?

"Nokummus." Addie said the name aloud, and the woman smiled, displaying blue and missing teeth. The girl wondered why she was to call her that instead of Miss Goodrich.

Then the woman said another surprising thing.

"I am here to help you. I will always help you."

Addie's first response was, "No. No, I don't need your help. I'm just fine. My family is fine."

But the woman held her with a gaze so deep that it penetrated to a place in Addie's mind and soul she herself had never entered. Under such scrutiny, Addie recognized something. She recognized it without a single doubt, and though this awareness made her suddenly weak, it somehow strengthened her. Nokummus — this woman who was a traveler from other realms as strange and unfamiliar as Chinese dynasties, this being who likened herself to a day star — held something powerful within her eyes, some knowledge that Addie would one day need to possess. Addie was certain, too, that the old woman would indeed be there for her as she'd promised and that she knew the truth, Addie's truth, the truth that she had hoped to keep as secret as a fallen tree in a silent forest.

*eight*

"THERE IS NO REASON TO FEAR," said Nokummus, and she raised her hands in a gesture that Addie interpreted as a peaceful sign. She didn't know how to reply but called out when the old woman turned to walk away.

"Where are you going? Don't leave."

"Do not fear," the woman said again, directing her voice ahead of her. She was moving swiftly now as if her moccasins floated over the frozen ground.

Addie stayed fixed to the spot where the two had come upon each other, and she waited until the Indian woman had crossed the field and disappeared into the trees. Why was she leaving if she planned to help her? If she thought that Addie needed help, surely she meant that she herself would be the one to give it. Was it those rough hands that had touched the bodies of her mother and brother and composed them for their final rest? Why had she done it? Where was she going? Where did she live? When would she be back?

When Addie approached the house, Fleur was out behind the barn, pushing her nose into bare spots in the snow. The cow mooed as the young girl swatted the heifer's flank to coax her back inside. "How did you get out here?" She knew she hadn't forgotten to close the barn door. Always mindful of keeping the animals inside while she was away, she clearly remembered how carefully she'd fastened the latch just this morning.

"What took you so long?" came a familiar voice she hadn't expected to hear. And she hadn't expected to see John Tower pushing the barn door open and grinning at her. "I thought you'd stayed after school again for sure. Gettin' to be a regular teacher's pet, I figured. When I stopped by the school to fetch you, Miss Fitzgibbon said as how your clock don't work."

"How you got here so fast is what I want to know," said Addie. "And why you came by in the first place." Addie had a shivery feeling at the thought of how he might have been here for a while and been poking around.

"I come to give you something." He paused to lead the cow into her stall. "And I noticed how Fleur and Little Star seemed kind of lonesome and needed fresh air."

Addie's eyes traveled to the morning's milk in the corner, now cold in the pail, and then to Little Star's empty stall. "Where is she?" she asked, and was in a panic until she ran back outside and found the horse standing in front of the place where the pine boughs covered the casket. If John had noticed anything strange, he wasn't saying. Since he hadn't been known to hold back information on anything that occurred to him, she relaxed a little.

"About that present," said John.

"You'd better keep it for your girlfriend, Fanny," chided Addie.

He looked mad enough to spit. He got all red-faced, but he didn't take the bait.

"This isn't a for-keeps kind of present," said John as he held out something dangling from a chain. It sparkled in the afternoon light. "In fact, there'll be heck to pay if Pa finds out I gave it to you, even for a little while."

Addie grabbed at the swinging object, and he released it into her grip. The back was smooth and shiny, but she could feel the tick of a clock mechanism through her fingers, and when she turned it over, the numerals shone gold against a white face.

"It was Pa's before he gave it to me," said John. "And he wouldn't want it loaned out."

She handled the pocket watch as if it were a hot potato and tried to pass it back to John. "I might lose it," said Addie. She couldn't take on the care of one more thing, even an object.

"I know," said John, "but how else you gonna get to school on time? Of course, I could go try to fix that clock of yours. You probably just need to know how to wind it up right."

"Not today," she fairly sputtered. Forcing a serenity she didn't feel into her voice, she added, "They're resting in the house."

"It is awful quiet. I knocked on the door and put my ear against it. Couldn't hear a thing."

"They sleep a lot."

"The fever's gone, though?"

"Oh, yes. It's gone. They're just so weak. You know."

"My ma was like that."

He pointed to the watch still in her hand. "You've got to wind it."

"I will."

"And don't show it off at school. Clive will know it's mine. He'd tell my pa."

At the mention of Clive, Addie thought about Demetry. Clive was the only one she could think of who would be mean

59

enough to kill her rooster. But why? There was definitely something about her that he'd hated from the start. And lately he'd acted as if she had the plague and meant him harm. But killing her rooster?

"Demetry's dead," she told John. All day she'd felt as if she had to tell someone.

"How'd that happen?"

"Don't know for sure. But I've got my suspicions. Clive told me once that a hen can't lay without a rooster about. Everybody knows you only need a rooster if you want some chicks. But he doesn't ever listen. He probably thinks we won't get eggs now that Demetry's gone."

Then she said, "Demetry's over there by the chicken pen. You want to take a look?"

John picked up the dead bird with both hands. It was so solidly frozen, it seemed as if it had never been alive. At first he turned it one way and then the next and wrinkled his forehead in puzzlement.

"There's a tiny slit down his neck," he said at last. "He musta bled to death."

They both were quiet for a while, and Addie hoped he'd leave before he asked more questions. Though deep down she dreaded the loneliness that would follow, she couldn't let her feelings show.

"Ground's too frozen to bury him," said John. "I'll take him with me if you want and throw him in the woods."

She didn't want Demetry thrown away. She needed things to stay as much the same as she could keep them. "Not yet," she said.

John shook his head. "My ma . . . the ladies hereabouts . . . they're wondering if . . . if there's something wrong. If your ma's as well as you pretend."

There it was. He *had* come to snoop.

"She's delicate," said Addie. "You know how she is. My ma's not like yours. She's delicate. And Jack, too. He's never been very strong."

"They'd like to come to call. The ladies. They'd like to bring out pies and things. And help you out some if you'd let them."

"Aren't they afraid of the contagion like Clive and his ma?"

"Not the ones who've taken to their beds already and are on their feet again."

"Well, we do appreciate the thought," said Addie very formally. "But a fuss like they'd be apt to make would likely cause a serious attack of nerves and set my mama back. I'll tell you when she's well enough for callers, John. I really will."

She said the last so dismissively that John began to back away, as if flustered that he'd said too much.

"They only want to help," he said, appearing hangdog and regretful as he climbed the fence and headed home. The moon was already in the sky, and as Addie watched him go, she wished with all her heart that she could call him back again and tell him everything.

*nine*

THE RHYTHM OF THE WATCH through her pillow kept Addie awake at first, then lulled her to sleep. When she next looked at it, the sky was just light enough for her to see that it was five a.m. Time enough to attend to the animals and get to school early.

John was there this morning but back in his regular place in front of Clive, who was still absent. Maybe the angry boy had taken sick just as he'd feared. Maybe she'd be blamed.

When Addie slid into her assigned seat, Fanny produced a peevish sigh that Addie chose to ignore.

The day seemed longer than most, with lots of busy work because of Miss Fitzgibbon's hoarse throat. Some of the time

Addie simply listened to the younger children read or told them stories to keep them quiet.

After school, she fully expected that John would be off to the yards. Mrs. Hardy had said how the push was on to finish another sharpshooter-type schooner by the end of the month. John did leave well before her but was waiting at the base of the small incline after the hearse house. She was so startled when he jumped down from the retaining wall where he'd been perching that she let out a little grunt of surprise.

"Thought maybe you were staying late again," he said as he brushed off his breeches and pulled his cap over his ears. Her book strap was full and over her shoulders, but he didn't offer to carry it, as if used to the idea that she would refuse such foolishness.

She was wary of having him come all the way to her house again and tried to think of shortcuts she could take and places where she could break away that would send him so far afield of his own destination that he'd leave her. But every turn she made, he was right on her heels like a devoted puppy.

"You don't need to go out of your way," she said at length. "I'm no little neighbor child you have to be watchful of."

He laughed, the light and tender sort of laugh she always liked to hear. It was bubbly on the end.

"You've never been no little neighbor child. What made you say a thing like that?"

"I mean, I'm nearly as strong as you, you know. I'm not some shrinking-violet kind of girl who can't fend for herself." She wanted to say like Fanny but kept quiet.

"Maybe not," he said. And then he stopped in his tracks and turned to face her. His sparky eyes seemed a tone dimmer. His mouth appeared to be waiting to receive the message they held. At last he said, "Maybe not until now."

"There's nothing different about now."

"There is. There's something real different. I'm not sure just what."

It was her turn to laugh, in a forced and lighthearted way she hoped would fool him.

He cleared his throat. "I looked into the windows yesterday."

"I keep the curtains pulled."

"There's places you can see through and in between."

"You are a snoop."

"And there weren't nobody moving in that house."

"I told you, John. They were asleep. You just don't listen, do you!"

"And no sound. No sound at all. Goll darn it, Addie, I know something's wrong. If you won't tell me what it is, who will you tell?"

Tell him? She'd wanted to from the very first. And he was right. There was no one else that she could trust. But would he keep the information to himself the way he'd need to for her plan to work? Or would he tell some grown-up, thinking it would be for her own good? She couldn't take that chance. But then he said something that struck terror through her like a lightning bolt.

"They're coming one day soon to see for themselves."

"Who? Who's coming?"

"The women. Some of their menfolk, too. I've heard my ma and pa talk about it. There's been rumors started by Clive's ma and some of the other ladies. They think there's something afoot."

"Why — why would they think that?"

"You won't let anyone come to call. I know your ma never got about much, but no one's seen her around for weeks, and yet you say she's better and you go to school."

"I told you that she's delicate."

"You did. You told me that. It's not enough."

Enough. What could she tell him that would be enough? "And proud," she added. "She doesn't like to ask for help."

"She's never had a problem in the past. My ma made soap for her the last two years because she feared the lye. And Mrs. Allen in Ipswich bakes her bread."

They were still out in the open meadow, but Addie felt for all the world as if her back was up against a wall.

"There's something wrong," said John when she didn't answer. "I know it just as sure as I know the night's about to come."

She bit her lip to keep back the words already forming in her head. She ran her tongue along her teeth and thought how it might feel to tell the truth to John, the same truth Nokummus seemed to know without a word from Addie. But John would need the details that she didn't want to speak out loud to any living soul. And — she could see it now — he'd need them soon.

The fence around her house was visible from where they'd stopped, and she took his hand and led him to it. They leaned against the rails awhile, scuffing their boots back and forth through the snowmelt at the base of the posts. She looked away and clutched herself around the stomach as if her arms could protect her from all that was to come. She let out a long sigh edged with resignation and a stifled sob, and she continued to look away from him, and then she spoke. She told him about the deaths of both Jack and her mother, of how she'd decided not to tell anyone, how important it was to her that she not be sent to live with a stranger. Finally, she described how she'd stolen a coffin, but she didn't say a word about Nokummus or about how badly Addie needed answers to the things that often claimed her restless mind and heart. When she was through, she gazed into his face and into eyes she didn't recognize, for all the dancing flecks were gone.

# *ten*

ONE DAY SOON. These were the first words to enter her head as she rose from a troubled sleep. John had said the people would be coming one day soon, and Addie didn't know if that meant today, tomorrow, the end of the week. When he'd left yesterday, he'd promised to take care of Fleur, Little Star, and the chickens if she were sent to live with some family in town. He'd actually said *when* instead of *if*, as though it were a foregone conclusion she'd be farmed out somewhere as soon as word got out that she was living alone.

In retaliation, she mentioned her wealthy uncle in Salem, the one everybody in the Ladies Aid Society must have heard of when Mama made her infrequent obligatory visits to this charitable group. She neglected to tell, however, how he hadn't contacted the family in years, clearly disapproving of his sister's lot in life. "He'll probably come for me in his buggy when he gets my message," she added. No need to say she hadn't sent him one and didn't intend to. In other ways she had told John the truth of things and tried to make him understand how she needed to live on her own until her father returned, but she kept the future parts, the possibilities that her contact with Nokummus had inspired, so closely to herself that she almost didn't dare examine them.

That morning as she fed the chickens, her eyes scanned the tree line for any signs of the old woman, her gaze traveling over the fields and meadows for as far as she could see in search of her. Addie had found nothing from Nokummus either inside or outside the house, no comforting sign that she was anywhere nearby and ready to help her. Such a wise person must know what Addie should do next. Maybe she would even have knowledge of when the townsfolk would descend. Why was she being so silent and invisible?

Addie milked Fleur, realizing that most of the milk would be wasted, for the cow had calved only a year ago and continued to produce enough for a family. The animal might prove to be a boon to John's household of many children, however, and Addie knew he would take good care of her. She patted the cow's broad sides and sang to her to ensure that her milk would flow undiminished.

At first she thought to stay near the house all day, but on impulse she saddled Little Star and rode her as far as the dunes in Ipswich that skirted the river on one side and led to the bay. The beach itself was long enough to give the horse a good run, but as they galloped along it, with Addie's head close to Little Star's neck and bursts of white sand flying from each hoof, she kept on the lookout for any sign of Nokummus and her canoe, the one Addie had sometimes watched her paddling in the river. They raced through scattered patches of ice and an invasion of empty quahog shells that covered the wet sand at the tide line. Surely the ancient Indian woman would be out collecting them as Addie and her father had seen her do before. Papa himself had often clammed for the large bivalves and brought them home to make chowder.

The woman's total absence from any of the places Addie suspected she might be caused the burning fear that had been building within Addie to settle in her throat and make her head hurt. She had thought she would find evidence of Nokummus somewhere in the fields and woods, and when she didn't, she was certain it would be here along this great expanse of beach. She was prepared to beg the old woman to tell her where she should hide, to ask for an amulet for her protection, to receive again the Wampanoag woman's promise that she'd be watched over. As gulls swooped and called, she naively listened for some mystical direction in their raucous shrieks.

But as another twilight approached, Addie had received no such reassurance. She trotted the horse back over the dunes and walked her the rest of the way, crossing the road and keeping as close to the trees as possible. Orange light from the setting sun filled the windows of her house in the distance and made it appear occupied and alive. She gulped a quick breath at the sudden thought that those people John spoke about might already have come and be waiting for her there. She pulled up on the reins and halted the horse while she squinted to catch any small movement and listened for any unusual sound that might be carried on the evening air. Not until she was convinced that what she was hearing were the accustomed noises of night creatures, and she was satisfied that nothing was stirring outside the house, did she continue on.

Such a momentary fright confirmed her decision to stop waiting for the events she'd been warned were coming and take an action of her own. If Nokummus wouldn't give her some guidance, as Addie had hoped, the girl would have to decide on a strategy herself, and she would need to do it as soon as possible, even though all the pieces weren't in place.

She debated for some time about whether or not to take the horse, finally deciding that Little Star would be better off in John's care than living by Addie's wits. And though she was uneasy at traveling a great distance in the dark, hadn't the night always been a friend to her and wasn't such travel overall the safest way? If she started off soon, she could reach the low-forested hills of the southern end of town well before morning.

Having camped with her father in all seasons, she knew what she would need to live out-of-doors in winter and prepared a sack of dried food and hard-boiled eggs and filled a canteen with water. She tried to think of this as just another adventure with her Pa, or like the time when she'd convinced him to let her camp out overnight in the woods by herself. For now, she refused to consider how long she might be gone or how lonely she might feel. After all, she reasoned, she'd been living alone here and had managed somehow.

Over her cloak she wrapped the warmest shawl she could find, one that had belonged to her mother but was so unlike anything else she had ever woven. The shawl was amazingly thick and had a bold pattern of deep colors from the natural dyes that Mama sometimes obtained from wild plum root, raspberries, and red maple bark but used sparingly. She rolled an extra woolen shirt, mittens, and a second pair of woolen breeches into a heavy blanket. A small pocketknife of her father's that she'd found in his wooden chest went into her haversack, along with a spade, a small saucepan, some hard candy, and a few dollar bills that he'd put aside for emergencies. She thought to leave John's watch for him to find but decided she might still need to know the time and slipped it into the pocket of her trousers. Finally, she tied up her thick hair and pulled the woolen watch cap over her ears.

Then carefully, as if she handled a prize piece of her mother's china, she took down the daguerreotype of the family that her father had commissioned shortly before he left for California. In it Papa looked proud and Mama was pale and small, with a tight smile. Fair-haired Jack, however, was grinning widely, and Addie noticed for the first time that she herself was looking intently into the camera as if she could see something on the other side of the lens. She wrapped the picture in blotting paper, then inserted it, the only image of all four of them together, between the packets of dried soup and wild berries, and she smiled to think that Papa had a copy of the same photo to look at from time to time — his happy family, the way they were just before he went away. Was there some busybody who would send an urgent message to him when they found his daughter missing? She comforted herself with the knowledge that even if he were traveling up the Pacific coast of South America by now, they wouldn't be able to reach him until he made land at California. Besides, a ship such as the *Metropolis*, carrying so many men on a mission, would surely not turn around to address a family concern of just one man.

On her way at last, she stopped at the casket and caressed the rim of it through the pine boughs. The townspeople would find it. But there was nothing she could do about that. Perhaps they'd put it in a covered place and, just as she had planned to do, keep it ready for burial in the town cemetery that had been her playground for almost seven years.

"Good-bye," she said so softly into the wind that the words were carried off like damselflies. Then she wiped her eyes, adjusted her burden, and began her journey across the snow-covered pastures.

The moonlight gave little luster, and when she looked back, she could barely discern her own tracks. Close to a clump of trees, the low hoot of a snowy owl caused her to drop her heavy load and search until she found the spooky bird on a nearby branch, motionless as a small rock and appearing to sit in judgment.

"What are you thinking?" she asked of the inert creature. "What do you know?"

As she rearranged her belongings and started off again, she glanced back across the clearing to the house she had left such a short time before and was stunned at what she saw. Lanterns bobbed through the yard and a dark form was leading her bellowing cow from the barn. Soon the hollow sound of calling voices began to reach her ears, and she started to run through the snow cover, a tight knot of panic and regret cradled in her chest as a rush of confused thoughts tangled her mind. Her instincts had been right, and she'd escaped the dreaded interference of the townsfolk just in time. It had been a real threat, and this was not going to be just another camping adventure.

She was grateful for the light snow that had begun to fall, for it would cover her footsteps. Those people were not apt to search for her at night, and by morning she would be someplace where they'd never think to look for her.

eleven

IN THE DARK, the usual landmarks were obscured, and Addie had traveled a few miles before she made a conscious effort to get her bearings. Fuzzy rectangles of light from a group of houses at the edge of the marsh told her she had not taken a wrong turn anywhere and was probably nearing the causeway. In minutes she could make out broad yellow circles of light from lanterns hung in some of the yards as well as the hulls of vessels looming like giants in the shadows. Their massive silent forms reminded her of the skeletons of mastodons she'd seen pictured in one of her father's books.

The lamps' warm radiance comforted her, even as she recognized that the quivering feeling in her gut was no longer so much fear as excitement. She was also filled with an unfamiliar sense of pride that she had conceived of such a bold plan all by herself and followed it through, at least this far.

There was not a soul or wagon on the causeway itself. The sky was darker than it had been just a short time earlier, so she knew it was coming on dawn and she'd need to hurry. She had penned a note that would support what John would have surely informed those busybodies by now and left it on the writing desk. It told how she wasn't in any danger and had gone to be with family — the uncle from Salem with the fine house and fortunate wife. John would also have said how he'd agreed to care for the animals. Of course, they might still be expecting her back at some point, and when she didn't return — well, that's when they'd most likely try to contact her kin or go searching for her in earnest.

She had a bumpy walk for a spell on frozen cord grass before crossing the causeway and heading to the river's edge. Seeing the outline of a newly framed vessel in the weak early light, she suspected she was by the Epes Story yard and still above the bridge. Luckily, the tide was low, and she could maneuver over a long stretch of ice-encrusted mud before being cut off by stacks of felled timber and a low fence. If memory served her right, there couldn't be too many other shipyards to travel through before she reached the place she was looking for. Her father had shown her the abandoned spot a few years back when he was looking to establish a business of his own. As with other enterprises that had occurred to him from time to time, there hadn't been enough money to pursue his vague plans.

She counted on the plot of land being unoccupied, for it was too small for the schooner trade, and operations for building smaller boats could do without the river on one side and the additional rent for such prime space. She remembered it was set back from the main yards and nearer the creek. But not until she finally stumbled into the familiar leeway, still cluttered with boat-building trash but otherwise vacant, did she relax her grip on her belongings and expel a steamy breath of relief into the frigid air, where it hung like a small cloud. Just as she recalled, there was a wooden lean-to some distance from the road that was filled in with snow. There were also an old model of a half hull, a broken auger and broadax, a collapsed steam box, and scattered trunnels. Too excited to be hungry, she rested on a pile of logs and tried to think of what she needed to do next. The dampness made the cold creep more deeply into her bones, and she felt as if she'd quietly freeze into the landscape if she didn't soon start to move again.

The unmistakable call of one loon to another startled her, and she wondered what those ominous-sounding birds were doing so far from their usual habitat much farther north. The eerie cries brought back that fearsome feeling she'd thought had left her, and, as she always did with natural phenomena she didn't understand, she pondered this occurrence as if it contained some sign.

"Papa," she said out loud as if she could conjure him, "I'm safe. Wherever you are, please think of me. I miss you so much."

This talking to herself was becoming a habit, but instead of adding to her empty feelings, it made her feel more in control and almost as if she had a companion. Today that companion would be her pa as she tried to reconstruct all the things she'd learned from him about surviving in winter. The many times they'd camped out together just for the sport of it, she'd felt privileged, for she'd observed that daughters in other families were rarely taken on such adventures. Her mother had objected at first, but one day acknowledged, quite grudgingly it seemed to Addie at the time, "Well, I guess. I mean, I suppose. That is, it seems to me it's simply what she's born to and in her nature. But I don't really see as how you need to encourage it." Addie wasn't sure what she'd meant by all of that, but afterward there'd been no more complaints.

She could now hear her father's voice saying, "Shelter first. Then comes water and then warmth." So first she would need to build a shelter more adequate than the lean-to, even though the existing weather-beaten structure might serve as a site and had a small roof. It was also on level ground and protected from the wind by some low conifers.

So after she'd brushed off the pile of logs and placed her haversack and other belongings on the driest part, she began scooping snow from the entrance. With only a spade, it was tiresome work, and she wasn't finished until the sun was full in the sky. By then the noise of hammering and sawing, the voices of the men in the yards beyond, and the hollow ring of timber as it fell could be heard. But she paid this little mind and sang nursery rhymes to lift her spirits, certain no one could hear her over the neighboring din and in her small space set so far back from the other yards. *Jack Sprat could eat no fat, his wife could eat no lean, and so betwixt the two of them they licked the platter clean.* Jack had liked that one especially and never tired of hearing it or the one about the crooked man who had a crooked stile. In love with the sound of the word *stile*, he'd never thought to ask its meaning.

As she worked, she piled the snow on the windward side to act as a windbreak and dug as close to the ground as possible, creating a deep snow trench. More than once the mound fell in on her, and she had to start again and pack it more tightly. When she'd finally finished, there were rivulets of sweat running down her face. She wiped them away with a stiff mitten and slithered inside the cavern she'd created to see if there was room enough to move about. Once her papa had shown her that even a candle could provide warmth in such a close space. With no candle and no smelly lucifer match like the ones her father used to light his pipe, she'd have to try another way to start a fire. She dug a small hole near the entrance to the shelter, then spent a long time finding something dry enough to use as a flint. Not quite by chance, for her quick eyes had scoured the place, she came across an old tin box by the broken fence. When she lifted the cover, she found wood scraps and twigs, which must have been protected from the elements for many seasons.

Much of this kindling went into her fire pit, and she chose the straightest stick to whittle to a point with her knife. Then she stuck the point into a groove in a piece of flat wood and rubbed the stick so hard that the friction finally birthed a tiny ember. Quickly, she dropped the ember into the nest of tinder and hoped it would catch. The first time it died in seconds. Other attempts proved fruitless as well. Finally, her hands so raw and cold she wasn't sure she could keep trying, another small ember emerged and a puff of smoke rose from the kindling to be followed by a thin blue flame. She hurried to place large stones around the edge of the fire, poured water into her saucepan, and held it over the growing blaze until it boiled.

Acutely aware of her hunger at last, she munched on a hard cracker while she waited, then emptied a package of soup into the pan and spooned it up, even though it burned her tongue. "*Soupa doopy loopy soupy,*" she sang when the last spoonful was finished, the same nonsense words that had always made Jack try a taste or sit back on his little haunches and laugh. The air was no longer filled with the clamor from the yards, and Addie's voice stirred the winter evening like a bird trill. But she was listening to her brother, his high giggle splashing like a brook over pebbles. When tears came, she didn't feel the wetness, just as she had become accustomed to the constant welling behind her eyes.

She had also stopped pausing to contemplate her losses or the ache that had become so much a part of her. Determined to continue to take whatever next step seemed to be the right one, she lifted the hot stones in her mittens, wrapped the edge of her heavy shawl around them, and climbed into the snow trench. Then she placed a blanket on the bare ground and slept, with the warm rocks pressed against her stomach.

It was still dark when she awoke, but her sleep had been so leaden that she couldn't tell if this was the same night in which she'd fallen asleep or if she'd slept away another day entirely. She crawled out a little ways to check the fire, which was still glowing. If this truly were the following night, some unseen hand must have added kindling and stoked it.

"Nokummus?" she called into the dark, but there was no answering voice and no rustle of clothing or sound of a footfall.

Still full of sleep, she made her way to the old privy that the previous occupants of this yard had left standing. It had been abandoned for so long that it smelled only of its cedar walls. When she returned and began to crawl back inside her shelter, she noticed the glint from the pupils of a small animal over by the woodpile. The form of it fell away in the blackness, leaving two bright eyes suspended in space. A *fox*, she thought at first, *or a young coyote*—some animal that might be as afraid of her as she was of it. Without moving from the entrance to her shelter, she peered into the dark and cocked her ears for any threatening noises from the small beast. But before she could even decide what it was, the furry body flew from its log perch and landed on the lean-to roof, sending a little avalanche of snow onto the fire pit that almost extinguished the flame.

*twelve*

A SINGLE PAW extended over the roofline as if it were fishing for something. It was larger than Addie had expected and had claws. Before she had time to react, the face of the animal itself appeared, whiskers twitching, and a sound she had never expected to hear in this place came from the open jaws.

*Meowwwwww!*

"Matilda!" screeched Addie as she lifted her arms to the cat, who was now off her belly and poised on the roof. She jumped into Addie's arms with no hesitation and snuggled there. "How did you find me?"

It wasn't the first time the cat had followed her. Twice she'd tracked Addie all the way to school, once waiting in the graveyard the full school day to travel back home with her. But Addie couldn't find any sign of her pet when she herself had run away, and she'd been certain that John would round up all the animals. Probably Matilda had disappeared into the woods and he'd thought he could retrieve her in the morning. Babbling with relief at finding her here, Addie held her so tightly that the cat had to struggle at times to remain settled in her arms. She rubbed her face against Matilda's and crooned to her while the cat's purring radiated through her like a tonic.

Food, thought Addie. What had she brought with her that Matilda could eat? As the cat wiggled from her arms to chase after something, Addie racked her brain to think of what human food the finicky cat might consider. She quickly broke off a hunk of cheese and held it out to where she'd seen Matilda disappear into the murk.

"Here, kitty, kitty. Here, kitty."

Where did she go? Surely she wouldn't leave after they'd just found each other? Addie was about to chase after her when the cat returned and crouched in the firelight, a live mouse dangling from her mouth. Preening with pride, she quickly vanished into the shadows again with her prize. It wasn't until early the next morning that she brought back a tiny mouse heart for Addie and put it at her feet.

"Thank you, Matilda," she said as she peeled a hard-boiled

egg and ate the cheese she'd saved for the cat. "I'm sure it's a delicacy, but I . . . I've already eaten breakfast."

As the days wore on, Matilda found other small prey and occasional dead fish at the river's edge, and Addie was so grateful the cat had followed behind and stayed with her. She'd been certain at first that Nokummus would show up at any time, but except for the one stoked fire, there had been no other indication that the Wampanoag woman was or had been anywhere near. Sometimes Addie wondered if it would have been so terrible to simply stay with a strange family for a while. There would have been a warm bed, hot food, people to talk to. But then she thought of Arabelle, the girl who'd been forced to take care of six unruly children she'd never seen before, or Jeremy, who worked so hard on the Colfaxes' farm that he hadn't been to school all year. Of course, this way she couldn't go to school either, but she was definitely on a real adventure, her adventure, and there was no one like Mrs. Spinny to tell her what to do. Thoughts of tending to such a bad-tempered lady all day long renewed her resolve. Still it troubled her that now that she had a really good and kind teacher like Miss Fitzgibbon, she couldn't profit from it or become her friend.

When Addie's water supply ran out, she collected water from the creek. At night she climbed fences to pilfer dry wood scraps from yards farther up the river, and during the day she hiked back into the woods to look for Nokummus. Tramping through the snow made her blood beat in her ears and was the only time she truly felt warm.

In time she learned to tread so quietly that once she followed a rabbit to its warren under the ground and a silver fox right to its den. Well past the pup-breeding season, there were older pups still living there. When the female sensed Addie's presence and began to pace at the entrance, Addie trekked back through the woods but returned many times to watch their progress. Soon she could identify the songs of some winter birds — the quick chortle of the northern flicker, the raucous scolding of the black-capped chickadee — and their warning and mating calls.

Sometimes a sudden flash of memory would bring her to a time when she had been very small and was carried in firm but soft arms. A voice had repeated words she didn't understand. There had also been much silence and sometimes the word *listen*. Sometimes the word *watch*. She remembered the warmth of the person who had held her, but not the face, for the life in the woods beyond had held her attention.

At length she would be distracted from this vivid recall by such things as the flicker of a bright red cardinal and his dingy red-crested mate, whose staccato chirps seemed to be asking questions.

And at times she felt so much a part of the wildness of the place that she could hear the whispers of animals and the earth breathing, and she would experience an unaccustomed and ancient peace. At dusk, however, the whinny of the eastern screech owl would send her quickly back to her shelter, where Matilda was usually sleeping inside.

She tried to keep count of the days, and she always remembered to wind John's father's watch and know the time. It made her feel more connected to the rhythms of the world she'd left behind. She knew for sure, of course, when Sunday came, because the shipyards were quiet and there were buggies on the causeway above her with families on their way to church. For a while a hard freeze made portions of the river look like a skating pond, and a sudden storm kept Addie inside her shelter both day and night. The yards were absolutely quiet then, and she felt like a hibernating bear, drifting in and out of sleep.

After one such storm, she emerged to find footprints, as large as a man's, all around the small yard. She had heard nothing from inside her shelter and saw only the prints of the person's boots, much too deep to have been made by moccasins. Surely this intruder had seen her snow shelter, but he or she had not looked in or disturbed it. For days she waited for the person's return or even for a group of people to descend upon her hiding place, and at times she was almost overcome by the urge to run away again and try to find an even more secluded spot. When after some time no one came, however, she stopped waiting anxiously and accepted the mystery for what it was.

And when her stores of food began to grow low, she decided it was time to try her hand at finding sustenance in the wild just as Matilda did. Since a diet of mice didn't appeal to her, she followed the creek upstream and foraged for mussels on the sandy bottom. Sometimes she broke a hole in the frozen marsh to find cattail and pond-lily roots and was rewarded with an occasional crayfish. But it was never enough, and she was learning the sharp pangs of hunger. Some days she was weak from it and found each movement an effort.

Coming back one evening from hours of foraging with little result, she was startled to find pieces of skinned rabbit turning on a spit over the fire.

"Nokummus," she called out at once. When there was no answer, she called the name again and again, running back and forth along the fence and even crossing the causeway to search for her in the woods. Frustrated at not being able to find the old woman, Addie took her time picking pocketsful of frozen high-bush cranberries before she finally returned to the shelter. When she did, the rabbit pieces were still roasting on the spit and a dark figure squatted by the fire. A terrified Matilda huddled near the privy.

# thirteen

THE FIGURE ROSE as Addie approached. In the flickering firelight, its long shadow crept all the way to the fence.

"Where'd you get such a skittish cat?" came a voice that broke the night quiet like a shaft of sunlight. "Tried to catch her after you left, but she woulda scratched my eyes out if I had."

"John," was all that Addie could utter at first. Her fingers inched around her throat as if she'd been struck dumb. After a pause filled with the sizzle and spit from the roasting meat, she added, "How'd you find me?"

"I'll bet you thought I didn't know about this place. Thought I'd be fooled like everybody else into thinking you really had gone to stay with your uncle."

When Addie didn't answer, he went on.

"Well, I will say I was all bothered up for a while there to think you pulled the wool over my eyes. About the uncle and everything, even though I'd never seen hide nor hair of him before." He stopped and poked a stick into a leg of rabbit. "You're a pretty good liar, Addie, but not a great one."

She'd never meant to be a liar at all. The fact that she was good at it was no point of pride. "I didn't want to lie," she said at last. "Especially to you."

"What I can't figure," he said as he turned to look her full in the face. If he saw her wet cheeks, he didn't let on, but he did begin to stammer some. "What I can't—I can't make any sense of is why you'd want to try to—to survive like this, out in the weather all winter long." He scratched his head. "And how you, a girl and all, fancied you could do it all alone."

Was he scolding her? Was that a trace of envy in his voice?

"It's no fancy, John," she said, keeping her eyes on the fire and not letting even a hint of a smile into her voice that would make her appear to boast. "I've been doing it. Surely you can see that for yourself. I've been doing it just fine." No need to tell him that she hadn't planned to exist out here alone, that she'd thought she would have Nokummus and the help the Indian woman had promised show up long before this. What she could admit to herself was that the thought that such assistance was just around the corner was what had kept her going. And when she stopped, as she did now, to take a good look at how she'd managed so far, she was pleased with herself and a little amazed.

"Well, you won't be so self-satisfied once the snow begins to thaw. You're just lucky the snow cover's been here longer than most years and your shelter's still standing."

She figured it was already way past time for a January thaw, but she'd forgotten to watch for it since the wall of snow she'd made only weeks ago had become as solid as ice.

"It's a little late in coming this year," John continued, "but the thaw's bound to be here soon. You can bet your britches on that." He looked flustered and began to stammer again. His eyes moved down to her feet. "You — you — *are* wearing britches. You're dressed just like a boy."

"I'm not meaning to look like a boy. I'm meaning to be practical."

"Doesn't matter what you're meaning. Girls and women. They're supposed to wear skirts. Everybody knows it."

"It's the circumstances that change the rules. My papa says that."

"What do you 'spose he'd have to say about these circumstances?"

"It seems to me," Addie began, and hesitated. How could she know what her father would think except by looking at how well she'd been able to use what he'd taught her? "I think he'd be proud of me," she said so softly that John had to make her repeat it. Even on a second try, the words were almost inaudible, as if she didn't dare to believe that John would agree with her.

There were still so many things she needed to ask him. And now that she'd been able to tell how she felt about things, she began a barrage of small questions. How were Fleur and Little Star? Did they take to being in with other animals? Had all the chickens survived?

The big question was hard to frame and so difficult to ask that she skirted around it until there was no other way than by blurting it out. "The casket. What about the casket?"

"They found it. Not the night they first came, but in daylight the next day." He took off his cap and held it between his knees, even though his ears turned near purple with the cold. "Nobody could understand it. How you'd put your kin to rest like that all by yourself. How you didn't tell a soul. They just kept shakin' their heads."

"Where is it now?"

"My pa and some other men moved the box behind the hearse house. They say there'll be a burial in the spring." That part was turning out exactly as she'd planned.

She imagined the schoolchildren playing around the cemetery, their shouts ringing in the chill and bouncing against the headstones. She thought of how Jack might have been one of those children one day and how, instead, all the footsteps at midday games would soon and for years to come reverberate into his grave.

A burial in the spring. Would she still be here in this shipyard in the spring? When they did put her mother and brother in the ground, would there be some way to say a last good-bye and not be observed?

"And there's another thing," said John. "There's been talk that there's a squatter in these abandoned yards. There's been some tools missing and a mess of trunnels."

"All I ever took were scraps of wood."

"Which means there might be someone else in hiding somewhere near."

"Or just some young'uns out larking."

"Either way, somebody's bound to come and take a look. Nobody'd ever think to find a girl out here, and no telling what would happen if they do."

She didn't understand why it would be worse for a girl and didn't know how to ask about it, sensing that John was talking about something she wasn't meant to know.

She'd been so careful, straying only to wooded places in daylight or foraging in the dark after all the workers had left the yards. How could anyone have seen her? When? Should she tell John about Nokummus? Was there anything to tell? Had he heard Addie call out the old woman's name? If he had, he wasn't letting on.

They sat in silence while John tended the rabbit. When it was ready, Addie had to summon what her mother used to call her polite appetite since she suddenly felt no natural one at all. A few bites of the tender white meat, however, made her hunger for more and forget her predicament, and soon she'd consumed two pieces down to the bones.

All the while, she was thinking how she had to ask another question that had been in her mind since John had arrived. "Do you maybe have a letter for me?"

"'Course I don't have a letter for you. The post don't come any quicker from California than the other way 'round, and your pa's ship is most likely still at sea. Last I heard, the *Metropolis* was figured to be somewhere near Valparaiso, wherever that is."

She had no idea. And it sounded so foreign and far away, she wanted to break down and cry against his shoulder. Determined not to, she said, "It's been so long," and held fast to each word, so her voice wouldn't quiver.

"Too long for you to be out here alone. I'm taking you back."

# fourteen

SHE WONDERED afterward how she'd been able to convince him to come back for her later. He'd been so determined that she go with him right away and had paced and tramped about as if trying to save her from a bear attack or a natural disaster. It was endearing in its way to have someone care so much for her safety, but there was an emerging awareness within her — and she noticed it more and more with each day out here alone — that there was a path she needed to follow, a hidden part of herself that she had to honor and explore, before she could go back to anything like the life she'd left behind.

"Just a few more days," she'd pleaded. "I'll be fine here for a few more days."

"And just what in tarnation makes you so dang sure of that?"

She could see that he was warring with himself, wanting to haul her off like one of his misbehaving brothers, but shying away from doing it when it was clear that she absolutely wouldn't budge. Still he huffed and cursed like a grown-up when he couldn't effect the rescue he'd obviously planned.

For the minutes it took for the dark to swallow his loping form on his way downriver, her eyes stayed fastened upon him. This time, she didn't want to bring him right back. Not yet. This time, her heart and mind were on a search for something that couldn't include him, and she didn't have the words to explain such certainty or the veiled knowledge that had caused it to lodge within her.

She awoke in the middle of the night feeling as if something as light as a butterfly wing had brushed across her face. She heard nothing but Matilda's purr and saw only the dying embers of the fire, framed in the entrance to her snow trench. Yet she knew without any doubt and with a complete absence of fear that she was no longer alone.

She held Matilda close as she shimmied from the shelter and straightened up to her full height. A yellow moon, high in the sky, cast a golden sheen over the yard, the creek, the monolithic vessels in the yards beyond and over a solitary shape that seemed to grow out of the landscape. Nokummus's long white hair flowed free, and she was enveloped in an aura of calm. As the stately old woman came toward her, Addie kept her distance, unsure at first if she should disturb such a powerful field of energy.

It was only when the woman spoke that Addie allowed herself to move closer.

"It is time," said the full, steady, and surprisingly warm voice that seemed to come from another time and place and had the resonant quality of a chant. Addie felt as if there was a specific answer she should have known to prepare—a chorus, even, that was meant to follow such a songlike proclamation.

What she did say surprised her, even as she realized it had been at the front of her thoughts and on the tip of her tongue for weeks.

"Where were you?"

"Near," answered Nokummus, as if it were a full and satisfactory answer.

Addie didn't think so. She had looked for her everywhere. And she'd been led to believe that this sage elder was going to help her. Misled was more like it, for she had counted on her help and it hadn't been there. "No," said Addie, and she pulled her shawl tightly around her and stood firm. She wanted to say that since she'd left home, she hadn't felt the woman's presence at any time in the way she had just minutes ago. "I didn't ever see you," she said instead. "I didn't ever . . . sense that you were anywhere around or even watching me."

Nokummus folded her arms across her midsection. Trinkets on her wrists jangled, and a sudden wind blew her hair away from her face, exposing deep wrinkles and a troubled frown.

"*Sense* can mean many things. It can take many forms."

Once again, Addie was confused by what Nokummus had said. She was beginning to feel very sorry for herself, an emotion she'd resisted for such a long time that now it threatened to envelop her. "You . . . left me alone when I . . . when I needed you."

The old woman shook her head. "Now," she said, and beckoned. "Now you need me. Come."

Come where? Where would they be going? Could she still trust her? If she did follow, what should she bring?

As if in answer to the last of her unspoken questions, Nokummus said, "Bring the cat."

In the distance, where the creek emptied into the river, a canoe was clearly visible in the moonlight. Nokummus must have navigated it here silently through the ice floes, and she was already walking back toward it.

"Where are we going?" asked Addie. She had to know. Why should she follow this person, wise though she appeared to be, without an answer to this very important question?

"Come," said Nokummus again, without turning around. She all but skated off in heavy mukluks over the frozen snow.

"I want an answer," demanded Addie. "You owe me an answer."

When there wasn't one, she remained standing for a space of time that seemed endless, her jaw set, her features pinched with disapproval, as she watched the mysterious Indian woman recede into the dark.

"Wait," Addie called after her when the moving figure was almost obscured. She grabbed the blanket, packed her haversack with what was left of her supplies, and held Matilda so closely that the cat released her claws. She only drew them in again as Addie, in her hurry to catch up, slipped and slid all the way to the water's edge.

"Here," said Nokummus as she handed her a smooth wooden paddle. "Put the cat in the boat." When Addie had done this and obeyed further instructions to kneel inside the canoe, Nokummus pushed the craft gently back into the river, entering it herself with an unexpected swift movement that belied her years. Soon they were slipping their paddles into the water with a rhythm that was precise, comforting, and almost familiar. At first, Matilda looked ready to leap from the boat but finally settled against Addie's left foot. Shadows of massive unfinished hulls lined their route as they traveled back closer to town and then pushed off toward the ocean through marsh grass and ice floes and into slicker, more open water.

Dark landforms emerged before them in silhouette, then moved mysteriously away as the canoe slipped past. Sometimes it seemed to Addie as if the landscape were in motion and they themselves were absolutely still, and after a while her arms began to ache from the constant dip and pull of the paddle. Sleepy from the cadence of it and too proud to admit her fatigue, she stared ahead and wondered when they would reach their destination.

"Soon," came Nokummus's voice from behind her, and Addie was surprised again at being understood without a word. A peculiar queasiness in her stomach, however, was making her feel desperate for landfall, and she was tempted to turn and say so. Fearful of upsetting the canoe's balance, however, she kept her head down and continued to paddle.

After a period of silence broken only by the swish of wood through water, Addie was conscious of cold beads of sweat across her skull and the rim of her forehead, and she began to shake uncontrollably. Heat radiated through her in sickening waves as if fueled from deep within. So dizzy that she crouched low to keep from tipping, the last things she remembered were letting go of the paddle, clutching her stomach in agony, and heaving up what seemed to be her very guts. Then darkness.

# fifteen

A RED-AND-BLUE PATTERN, very like the one woven into her mother's heaviest shawl, threaded in and out of Addie's consciousness. She would sleep and wake and sleep again, with the geometric design traveling through her fuzzy thoughts as if it were an important blue sky or a far-off horizon or a resplendent rainbow she couldn't quite grasp. When finally her eyes managed to stay open, they were in fact fastened upon such a pattern. It decorated a finely woven bulrush mat that trailed up the curved sides of a strange enclosure and was right next to her head. Still dizzy but finding that she could raise herself on her elbows, she searched the small space for anything familiar. A flap of what seemed to be a sheet of birch bark blew in and out over an apparent entrance, and smoke from a small fire pit rose through a hole in the roof. Deerskins covered her, and the fur was stiffer than Matilda's against her fingers. Odd-looking cooking implements were placed near the fire, and there was a bubbling pot hanging over it from a crude support of sticks. It was filled with something that gave the entire room a pungent odor and made Addie sneeze. Where was she? And where was Matilda? Why was Addie lying on this hard pallet, and why was she alone?

As she ran her tongue over her teeth to discover the reason for the awful taste in her mouth, the bark flap parted and Matilda shot through it.

The words "Such a bad sickness" seemed to come from the cat until Nokummus entered and it was clear that the exclamation had belonged to her. On seeing Addie so wide awake, the old lady's lips parted in a crooked smile accented by a few dark and missing teeth.

"Bad sickness," she said again, and shook her uncovered head. "Bad meat." She held up wild roots. "But I made you some good medicine."

The only meat Addie had eaten had been the rabbit. If it was John's rabbit that had poisoned her, it must have done the same to him. She hoped he was all right.

Addie didn't want to swallow some curious concoction, especially now that she was feeling stronger. At the same time that she was wondering how long she had been here, she was thinking of ways to resist Nokummus's potion.

"My *wetu*," said Nokummus, moving her free hand in an arc that mimicked the shape of the space.

"House?" asked Addie, and Nokummus nodded.

It was very small, but cheerful and warm. A *place*, she thought, *in which Jack would have loved to play.*

"Where are we?" asked Addie.

"On the big island."

Addie knew the names of the islands but had never been on any of them. Hog Island was the largest, but there was also Long Island and tiny Corn Island before you came to Essex Bay. Nearby Cross Island would have taken no time at all to reach from the yards, so she decided this must be Hog. The Choate family had owned a farm here for years and years. She'd also heard of two other small farms and a cheese maker who plied his trade on one of them. She wondered if the Choates lived in the old house in winter and if anyone was aware of an Indian squatter nearby.

"Medicine," Nokummus said once more. She ladled some of the mixture from the pot into a small pottery bowl and held it to Addie's lips.

When Addie shook her head, Nokummus pressed more firmly until the girl was forced to take a sip or fall back onto her sleeping platform. The thick liquid had a peculiar flavor, but even a small amount caused an immediate calming effect on her churning stomach.

Apparently satisfied with her ministrations, Nokummus sat cross-legged on a pile of blankets, picked up an unfinished basket, and began to twine dried grasses. The action was reminiscent of the times when Addie's mother would sit and weave, so engrossed that sometimes Jack's or Addie's voice couldn't penetrate her trance. And yet the unfamiliar surroundings, the low humming while the old woman worked, the closeness of the sounds of the wild, and the lapping of the waters of Essex Bay made Addie feel completely removed from that other place, that other life. Except for the pattern in the bulrush mat and the voices of the woods and sea, there was nothing familiar here. Still—and this she couldn't understand at all—there was nothing overly strange. She didn't feel as if she'd stepped into another world or some foreign place. The deer hide against her skin felt right; the low light and strange odors sparked partial memories that slipped in and out of conscious thought.

Nokummus removed the small pot from the fire and replaced it with a larger one filled with snow. In a very short time, the snow had become warm water, and she handed Addie some torn pieces of cloth.

"You must wash your body now," she told her, and then helped her remove the layers she'd been wearing for weeks.

She gave her a simple deerskin dress, collected the soiled garments, and started out the doorway. "I will clean your clothing."

Later Addie would learn that Nokummus pounded the garments with snow and dried herbs, and scraped them with deer bristles. For now, she was relieved to wash away the sweat from the fever and to feel her skin breathe again. The deerskin dress was warm and ample. Since it was obviously too narrow for the Indian woman, Addie wondered who it had belonged to. And though still weak, she felt cared for — better cared for than she'd been for a long, long time. Tears were again very near the surface, and she did nothing to stop them from spilling over. Nokummus returned shortly with potatoes and root vegetables and soon made a fragrant stew. After eating what little she could, the still-weakened Addie lay back on her pallet, ready for sleep, but Nokummus beckoned her closer to the fire.

"It is time for a story," she said, cross-legged again and with her strong brown hands entwined in her lap. "The Wampanoag people know many stories."

A story. No one had told Addie a story in years. Jack had loved the ones she made up, and Papa had often said she had a gift for telling them. Had she come to this place to hear stories? It was such a fanciful thought, it almost made her laugh out loud.

The old woman gave a long sigh. She tapped her forehead as if waking something inside. Her eyes were wide but focused inward. Addie found herself sitting erect with anticipation.

"The Wampanoag have lived near here always. Always."

When Addie didn't respond, Nokummus continued. "Before the white man." She became very still and quiet as if trying to remember. After a long hesitation in which Nokummus murmured to herself and Addie had begun to fidget, the woman started in again, this time with a very long story about Moshup the Giant, who lived in Massachusetts before the Europeans came. She told how he caught whales and shared the meat with other Indians, how he predicted the coming of men with pale faces. She told about the Makiaweesug, the Little People, who lived in the woods and had magical powers, and about silver flutes and medicine clowns, her voice droning on and on like a lullaby. Though Addie fought sleep, because she really did want to hear it all, at length her eyes began to blink open and shut, open and shut, until they finally closed on the colorful world of the Wampanoag, even as Nokummus continued to paint it with a slow and graceful brush.

# sixteen

IN THE FEW DAYS THAT FOLLOWED, as Addie began to help Nokummus with tasks around the *wetu*, she closely observed the way her capable fingers, in spite of their swollen knuckles, performed such fine movements as were needed to grind dried herbs and weave baskets. Though Addie was quick to learn new skills, she often missed her books and thought about the school and how it was only a short distance away on the mainland. Knowing that it was nearby, even though separated from them by an inlet, made her especially homesick for it, for the lessons she was missing, for the kind interest of Miss Fitzgibbon. When she mentioned this to Nokummus, the woman nodded and put down the leather breeches she was mending.

"I went to school," she said. When Addie looked surprised, she continued. "On an island. South from here. Where my Chappiquiddic tribe lives."

"A regular school?" asked Addie. She had thought that Indians didn't need or want things like that. That they learned from the land. Yet the old woman's English, though somewhat abrupt at times, was so clear that Addie knew she must be telling the truth and had at least had schooling in letters.

Nokummus laughed. "There was no building that said *school*. We sat cross-legged together inside a large *wetu*. What is called a *neesquattow*. We had a special white-man teacher. Mr. Baylies." She said the name reflectively, as if he had been someone of great importance in her life. "Good teachers make good students."

"I have," Addie began, but corrected herself. "I had a good teacher. Her name is Miss Fitzgibbon."

"Yes."

"You know Miss Fitzgibbon?"

"I have studied her."

It seemed an odd answer. Addie wanted to ask why or for what purpose. When she came right down to it, why was this Indian woman living so far away from her own tribe? Why did she live out here all alone, and why was she now so willing to help Addie, after ignoring her for so many weeks? This last was at the head of her many questions, and the one that hadn't really been answered when Nokummus had come for her. Suddenly, completely out of context with the present conversation, she blurted it out. "Remember how you promised to help me that time we met in the field? Why did you leave me by myself for so many weeks? Why didn't you come any of those times I called out to you?"

Nokummus continued sewing and didn't look up. But Addie noticed a slight quivering of her chin. One eyelid twitched. "It was not easy to allow you to learn," the old woman said at last. "Not easy to wait."

"Learn what? Wait for what?"

"Learn to live by your own mind." She rubbed her forehead. "Own . . . wits. Learn to be a creature of earth, close to the deep heart of the world."

Creature of earth. "But I was cold. I was hungry."

"Like the wolf. Like the fox."

"But I'm not a wolf or a fox."

"Not an animal?"

Addie had to admit that often in that snow-covered landscape, crouching in her shelter or foraging for food, she had felt very much like any other creature in the wild and curiously attuned to each one.

"It was another kind of school," said Nokummus, and she rose abruptly, put on her cloak, and left the wetu.

These sudden excursions would sometimes happen many times a day, but the Indian woman usually came back with something important—corn and squash from her garden that she had dried or stored nearby, kindling for the fire, a report on the weather, a prophesy of events to come. The girl could not stop wondering why this elderly Wampanoag lived so far from her tribe, completely dependent on her own devices. Had she been turned out for some reason—murder or worse? Addie had heard tales of such things, Indians sent to wander because they had violated some code or sacred precept.

Now that she was feeling stronger, Addie decided that she would soon begin to follow her. But for a little while longer, she'd simply accept the warmth and safety here. Matilda could not stop purring, even during the interruptions to her nap when she moved only to arch her back and stretch.

This time when Nokummus returned, the woman seemed pleased.

"The thaw is here," she pronounced. "Soon we will search the island. We'll make use of a second pair of eyes. Young eyes."

Did Nokummus have trouble seeing? Had she lost something? Had she brought Addie here to help find it? In daylight, the old woman's eyes did often appear cloudy. The right lens was in fact milky and dull. Yet she went about her daily rituals as if her vision was perfectly clear. Addie began to watch the way she compensated with the use of her other senses, especially the sense of touch. She stroked objects and held them up to the light. She often extended a hand or walking stick ahead of her. In the dark, her hands reached out to either side, even as her movements continued to be swift for someone so old. Of course, Addie could only judge her age from the somewhat wizened and weathered appearance. Up until now, her only reference for anyone of advanced age was old Mr. Perkins, who had recently celebrated his seventieth year, or Miss Crowell, the maiden lady in town who took in boarders and bragged of being nearly eighty. Both moved slowly, and neither was nearly as spry as this Indian lady.

Addie was aware that *lady* was not a term that others would have used for her new companion. Her mother was a true lady, as both parents and occasional folk at the meetinghouse had often reminded Addie. Refinement, breeding, accomplishment in the womanly arts, grace — these were what true ladies possessed, and, sadly, they defined areas in which Addie always seemed to fall short. Yet, she pondered, there was such grace to Nokummus's every movement, such a sense of purpose, so many skills for living that she'd mastered. Only yesterday, Addie had watched, amazed, as she constructed an intricate small animal trap from twigs, branches, hair, and some kind of fiber. The differences between the two women were stark, however. For instance, Mama had used a parasol when outdoors in sunlight; Nokummus seemed to invite the elements to color and etch her skin.

That night, after a supper of cornmeal mush and dried berries sweetened with honey, Nokummus again began to tell stories. The first, why the cricket is black, took only a minute to tell and made Addie chuckle to think of a cricket laughing so hard at the joke of a mosquito that he fell into a blazing fire. The storyteller's own laugh rumbled low in her chest and escaped through her nose in quick snorts. When these subsided, she began long rambling accounts of changelings and shape-shifters and the Makiaweesug again, one of which had once boldly entered a *wetu* at night to ask for help. "He is such a small person," said Nokummus, "that the woman of the *wetu* thinks he must be a boy, and she goes out into the darkness to follow him."

Her words were sonorous and slow, full of mystery. "There is no wind." She sighed and spread out her hands. "So little light from the moon that the woman must move with swiftness not to lose track of the boy. Her husband calls out to her, 'Do not go,' but she hurries faster until the smoke from the *wetu* is far, far away." Nokummus's voice, rhythmic and low, paused now and then as she took in breath and slowly expelled it. "The boy takes her to another *wetu*, where she finds a sick and very small woman, and this makes her know she is with the Little People and the boy is a little man. 'Please cure my wife,' says the little man. His wife moans and cries, and the Wampanoag woman comforts and tries to heal her." Nokummus began to chant like a medicine woman and shook her hands over the fire, casting frantic shadows onto the bulrush mats. "The Indian woman stays until the little wife is well. The Makiaweesug give her many presents for thanks. They put a blindfold on her eyes and lead her from the hidden place and back to her own *wetu*."

"Did she know where to look for them again? Did she ever find them?" asked Addie, her words so full of sleep they tumbled over each other.

"Never," said Nokummus. "She looked and looked, but she never found the secret place."

Addie rubbed her eyes to keep awake, even as she kept slipping in and out of the old woman's story. When the melodic voice also began to drift with weariness, Nokummus brought her tale to an abrupt halt and cleared her throat in an apparent effort to make certain that Addie was awake and that she had her complete attention.

"Tomorrow," she said solemnly, and brought her hands together in a prayerful gesture. "Tomorrow we begin an important story, an important search."

There was that *search* word again. What did she mean? What could she possibly be searching for on Hog Island, and why was it so important to her?

# seventeen

THERE WAS NO LIGHT in the *wetu* when Addie opened her eyes. The coals in the fire pit glowed orange, and soft snores came from Nokummus's bed. Matilda, too, was asleep. The presence of these others made Addie feel both less lonely and freer than she'd been for many weeks. It was as if she'd dropped anchor in a safe harbor, sure that she could pull it up again when there was a need. She couldn't imagine what that need might be, just as she could never have envisioned any of the events of the months just past or how deep and uncertain the divide from her father would feel as he traveled so far from her. She allowed her thoughts to go back to the recent days in the cold shipyard. Maybe Nokummus had been right to let her struggle there alone. This new sense of freedom, would she have found it if she hadn't had to earn it?

If she turned on her back, she could see one bright star through the hole that released smoke from the fire. Framed by the night, it seemed to be watching her. Did any of the changelings and ghosts Nokummus told about live in the sky? Where did the ghosts of children go? In her mind's eye, she watched Jack skipping from star to star. Star to star.

It seemed she hadn't had time to do more than blink before the round room was admitting morning light through the birch flap, and Nokummus was cooking flat corn cakes and frozen smelts. The tiny fish were crisp and salty. After the satisfying meal, Addie warmed her hands on a bowl of huckleberry tea. Already the gulls, more raucous here than upriver, were announcing the day. When she left the *wetu* to relieve herself in the underbrush of the hillside, the ice patches were soft under her feet and spots of bare earth were beginning to show through what was left of the snow. She didn't feel the need to pull her shawl so tightly around her. Though the thaw seemed sudden, she realized it might have already begun when she first arrived here, and she knew from years past that it could sometimes last a week.

She climbed all the way to the top of the drumlin, where she could watch thin rivulets run down the path leading to the Choate house. No smoke came from the chimney, and most of the windows were boarded up for the winter, a clear indication that the family would not be back until spring or summer. A large chimney rose from the center of the roof, and an empty porch stretched across the front of the whitewashed summer home. A white picket fence followed the curve of the downhill slope to the stream below. Two young elm trees framed the well, and an empty swing hung from a crooked chokecherry and blew back and forth in the wind.

Addie hiked down to the large barn, and as she eased open the door, she half expected to find swallows in the rafters above the haymows. In summer it would be a perfect nesting place.

There was only one other habitation on the island, except, of course, for Nokummus's *wetu*. She'd seen a man come and go from the little farm north of the Choate land and had even come across him on the path one day. He'd looked at her quizzically as she darted past him but did nothing to acknowledge her. Addie wondered if he knew about the wigwam.

Back inside the *wetu*, she had to ask, "When did you build this place? How did you do it?"

"The same way as ever."

Addie waited for her to continue. After a while she said, "But I don't know what *as ever* means."

"As did my ancestors."

"There are so few trees here. How did you make the frame and sleeping platforms?"

"At the end of one summer, I brought saplings from the forest on the mainland in my canoe. I made many trips. Sassafras for poles. Sweet birch for hoops. Cattails and bulrush from the river for mats."

Addie's eyes traveled over the interior, where she could see evidence of all the materials Nokummus spoke about. It would have taken such strength to bring them here and put them in place. It was hard to believe that this woman before her possessed it. She was not much taller than a girl, weathered as an old tree, and slightly stooped, but Addie knew without any doubt that it must be so.

"We begin now," Nokummus said suddenly. She wrapped a light shawl around herself and put on a pair of moccasins, leaving the heavier mukluks behind. Addie followed her outside, where the earth seemed to be breathing in long, barely audible sighs as warmer air loosened the hard grip of winter. There was so little wind, she had to shake her long hair to feel it move freely. The strands sifted through fingers that today, without mittens, didn't ache from the cold.

"Time for the earth to wake a little. To stretch," said Nokummus as she bent to brush snow away from the withered fruit of a beach-plum bush. She held a long stick and touched it to the ground as they went. Addie thought the stick looked like a divining rod used by someone hoping to find water. Papa had hired such a person before he'd dug their well.

As they moved away from the *wetu*, she could see clearly now that it was built close to a small channel that emptied into the bay. The canoe was pulled up onshore, where fat winter snipes foraged on bands of barnacles, their yellow stick-legs in constant motion. As her father had once described it, the beach was thick with quahog and oyster shells left by the Agawam Indians who'd lived here many years ago. Farther away, three dark cormorants perched on the rail of some kind of wharf, a place where the Choate family probably docked a boat when they came in the summer. On the long climb back up the drumlin, Nokummus stopped every little while to trace bare places with her stick and scratch those still crusted with snow. She had not yet called upon Addie to scrutinize anything with her clearer vision, but if it was a small object she had lost, how could she possibly find it, the girl wondered, in this expanse of wild land on this largest of the islands?

After they'd trekked in this manner all the way to the hilltop and down to the rock outcroppings, Addie ventured to ask, "What are you looking for?"

The old woman continued to scratch the earth and didn't answer for some time. When she did, Addie felt no better informed.

"The spirits will be the guide. Earth will tell the story."

"What story?"

"We can't know the story until we find the place of the answer."

It sounded like a riddle to Addie, and she didn't feel inclined to help when she had no idea what they were looking — searching — for.

A pale sky tinged the color of apricots made it seem like another season entirely, and Addie longed to run down the path, whooping and hollering, leaving Nokummus to pick about by herself as if she were looking for gold. Actually, Papa had explained the way in which you panned for that valuable mineral, and she wondered if he was anywhere near his destination yet, if he was even close to traveling into the California hills with a pickax and donkey, as he'd described. Receiving a letter from him had become an impossibility. Even if one did come to the post office, there was nobody now — not even John — who knew where to find her. Acknowledging this fact made her feel adrift again, and she doubted the reasons for being here with this person who was little more than a stranger. What had made Addie so certain that the Indian woman held answers to monumental discoveries about herself? Had Nokummus really promised to reveal them? How had she conveyed this message that now seemed as deeply ingrained as a mark of birth?

"We will return tomorrow," said the old woman. She put both hands on Addie's shoulders and turned her away from the path to face the bay. "The spirits are not ready."

"Ready for what?"

This time Nokummus merely shrugged as if she'd grown weary of Addie's many questions.

The story she told that night was different from any of the others. There were no ghosts or changelings, no magical fish or silver flutes. It was a real world, a tribal world on another island where a young girl lived with her mother and brothers.

"This girl passed many tests, and grew into a beautiful and wise young woman. Some thought she would be a *pauwau*, that she would make the Wampanoag people very proud."

"What is a *pauwau*?" interrupted Addie.

"A healer. What some might call a medicine man or woman."

"And did she become one? Did she do anything great like that?"

Nokummus shook her head. The firelight accented the deep wrinkles of a frown.

"You must listen to the story. You must wait for the answers."

Addie settled back onto her sleeping platform, a fist against her mouth as a reminder to keep her thoughts to herself. For reasons she didn't fully understand, she desperately wanted Nokummus to finish the story. It took such a long time for her to begin again, however, that Addie started to think she'd already spoiled things. She closed her eyes and waited behind dark lids, fighting sleep and anticipating the sound of that comforting voice.

Slowly, choosing words with her usual precision, Nokummus did begin again.

"A white man came to the island. A boat builder. A friend of the Wampanoag. They hired him to teach the men his craft so they could build larger vessels. He taught the young woman with nimble mind and hands how to caulk seams of the boats."

Addie couldn't stop herself. She had to know. "Did they . . . did the girl and the man fall in love?" She hoped they had.

"Yes," said Nokummus. "But love stories are not always happy."

Tears glistened in the old woman's eyes.

*Don't cry,* Addie wanted to tell her. *It's just a story.* But seeing Nokummus's extreme distress, Addie suddenly realized that it wasn't.

# eighteen

ADDIE HAD HEARD that Hog Island got its name because it was shaped like the fat back of a hog. But how was it possible for anyone to observe the contours of it except by arriving from the ocean side or falling from the sky? While the warmer weather still held, she climbed again to the top of the hill. Across the river to the north was the wide stretch of dunes she'd traveled through with Little Star. She hoped the gentle horse was being ridden often by John or his brothers and sisters. This island would have been no place for her. Even Matilda seemed more skittish with water on every side. The cat was playing hide-and-seek by darting from leafless bush to bush.

The tide was out, and to the west Addie could clearly see what looked to be another very small island in the river. It sparkled and shone through a fine mist that hovered above it. She quickly decided that if she hurried before the tide came back in, she could easily reach it on foot, so she slipped and slid down the hill until she came to the water's edge and the stony path that joined the two pieces of land. The plot itself was little more than a mound of stones. As Addie sifted pebbles through her fingers, she marvele d at the shine and smoothness of some of the larger stones and how carefully they seemed to have been placed. She was amazed to find that on closer inspection there were objects among them that appeared to be arrowheads and tomahawk heads. Collecting what she could carry, she ran back across the narrow causeway just as the tidewaters were inching over it, and she hurried to the *wetu* to show the booty to Nokummus.

"Look what I found," she said as she deposited her treasure at the old woman's feet. Nokummus was squatting as she sewed and at first didn't look up from her work or down at the handful of objects. When she did, her eyes became dark and enraged. She put her hand to her throat and sank her nails into the loose skin. "What have you done?" she exclaimed.

"There's a place," Addie began to explain, "a tiny island."

But Nokummus cut her short with angry words. "It is a sacred place. It is holy ground. It is not a place for a young girl to play."

"I wasn't playing."

"Or remove sacred relics." She carefully pushed the stony pile away from her before gathering the artifacts into a basket and covering them with a small blanket. "At the next low tide, you must bring them back. You must say a prayer of regret to the ancestors of the Agawam whom you dishonor."

"I didn't mean . . . it didn't seem . . . the stones . . . I didn't think it was a graveyard."

"It is a very old Agawam burying ground. In summer, members of the tribe still come to give homage, gather sweet grasses, bring gifts." Her eyes burned with a fury Addie hadn't seen in them before. Nokummus gave a forceful grunt of disgust. "The dead must never be disturbed."

Addie cringed at first at the force of Nokummus's anger, but then began to silently rebel, thinking how she hadn't meant any harm and didn't deserve such a dressing-down. Maybe she should rethink what she was doing out here in this remote spot with this peculiar old Indian woman. Maybe she should just leave.

But when Nokummus remained unusually quiet after her outburst and ate very little at the evening meal, Addie began to feel protective of her and contrite. A sudden snow squall at nightfall caused the old woman to stiffen and pull her shawl tightly around her. She pinched her lips into a tight and trembling line as she quickly fastened the birch flap and backed up against the entryway as if to keep the storm at bay. Her voice was low and fearful.

"The ancestors are troubled."

Those were the only words Nokummus spoke that evening as the wind swirled against the cattail mats and made the eel grass in the seams squeak. There was no continuation of the story about the beautiful young woman, and Addie felt as if she herself had lost her voice. She didn't know how to explain away this terrible transgression, and she dreaded the morning when she'd need to travel back to what she knew now must be a haunted place.

The lowest tide of the following day occurred sometime later than when she'd first found the little island. She hadn't even looked at John's father's timepiece since she'd arrived here with Nokummus, and she'd become content to be completely dependent on the rhythms of their life here and her growing sensitivity to the changes in light and tides and the churning of the world. The river had washed away most of the snow cover from the storm, and the mound of stones gleamed in shafts of early sun like one jewel with many facets. The mist that had engulfed it was no longer there, but the small island continued to seem set apart by something more than just distance. Knowing the history this time, she was burdened with a strong foreboding and stumbled across the barely exposed path.

The basket she carried seemed much heavier than its meager contents would suggest. She didn't know where or how to begin returning the artifacts and felt like a criminal coming back to the scene of a crime. As she stood quietly collecting herself, however, the fear began to lift and an unexpected sense of peace drifted over her like cobwebs. In its hold, she bent to cautiously scatter the relics in much the same random way she had accumulated them. In her mind she began to form the prayer of regret and apology that Nokummus had demanded, releasing the halting words into the air when her mission was complete.

"O, most ancient ones," she began. She knew that *Dearly departed* is what the preacher would have intoned, but Addie figured this occasion required a greater form of respect. "I have returned with the sacred relics that belong to you. They're all here. See? I meant no disrespect, and I'm very sorry to have disturbed your final resting place."

She tried to imagine the Indians who were buried in this strange graveyard with no markers and was conscious of their invisible eyes upon her. Were they warriors, chieftains, or ordinary members of a long-ago Agawam tribe? Were their bones, in fact, still underneath these mounds, or had they crumbled and sifted away like sand? But as hard as she tried, the only picture she could draw to mind was of her mother and little brother locked in an eternal embrace and waiting for burial. This unexpected and vivid memory brought her to her knees on the wet stones, where she shook with sobs in the grip of her own arms.

Still shaken as she turned to leave, she looked across at Hog Island and at the figure of Nokummus high on the ridge of the hill and scrabbling through the snow cover with the tip of her stick. The storm had brought colder air, and it seemed to Addie that they should both be indoors by the fire and not battling the wind that continued to punish anything in its path with icy blasts. Yet even though she still couldn't guess what Nokummus was searching for, she knew it was futile to encourage her to stop, and it didn't seem right to leave the old woman to search alone. So, once back on the island, she mushed through the thin layer of new snow all the way to the hilltop, calling out as she approached so as not to alarm the old one. Only the night before, the cry of a wolf had pierced the silence, but Nokummus hadn't stirred. Oddly, at other times, the faint whir of a swarm of winter moths might grab her attention.

Nokummus held her arms tightly at her waist like a barrier as Addie approached. She watched the young girl come toward her as if the child were bent on delivering an ominous message. That she was coming only to assist her appeared to be something the woman could not comprehend at first, and she bristled when Addie drew near. At the sight of the empty basket, however, she visibly softened. The space between her heavy eyebrows grew wide with relief.

"I did what you said," said Addie, wishing that the old woman would embrace her and say that she was pleased and all was forgiven. But there was no move of any kind in Addie's direction, and she had to settle for a more welcoming expression on the weathered face and in the eyes that weren't so shadowed with concern. Their clouded gaze immediately reached over Addie's head and down to the distant Agawam burial ground as if to make certain that peace had been returned to it and any vengeful specters subdued.

"Let me help you look for . . . whatever . . . for anything . . . you're looking for," said Addie.

Nokummus moved the stick from one hand to the other. Her deep sigh turned to smoke in the frigid air. "The sleeping earth provides no signs."

"Signs of what?"

"Of what it holds. It will be better in springtime. Better in summer."

Addie rebelled at the thought of still being here by themselves in spring and summer, still searching for something Nokummus refused to name. She'd hoped that her father would be back home by then and that she, too, could return there. "If you'd just tell me," she all but shouted. "I'll bet you wouldn't have to wait so long. I'm really good at finding things."

"Things," said Nokummus coldly. "We are not looking for things."

"Then what are we looking for?" Addie asked. Noting that the old woman had used the word *we*, she repeated her question.

Nokummus started back down the hillside. She spoke her words into the wind as she moved away, and Addie had to run after her in order to collect them.

"Tonight I will tell more of the story. I will give you answers to questions you do not yet know to ask."

# nineteen

A HEAVY STEW of root vegetables and dried wild turkey made Addie so sleepy that she wondered if she could stay awake for the promised story. That afternoon, thinking she might have injured herself in climbing over a fence or a felled tree, she'd decided to tell Nokummus that some days ago she'd found bloodstains on her undergarments. She hadn't wanted to make such a revelation and was secretly afraid there might be something terribly wrong with her. But the old woman had seemed curiously overjoyed with the news, telling Addie that this bleeding from a woman's body was a sign of power and deep connection to the earth, that it was a natural occurrence in preparation for the bearing of children and an indication that Addie had become a woman herself. She said it was something to celebrate, that she herself was prepared to be her guide during this important time.

Addie had been nervously reflecting on all of this ever since, and during the time it took for Nokummus to put things in order again after the meal, she was revived by a walk outdoors to clean the cooking implements and a curiosity that had been building for days to know the rest of the love story. Returning, she sat cross-legged on her pallet and tried not to fidget as Nokummus poked around the *wetu* and hummed tunelessly under her breath. Just when Addie felt she might explode with anticipation, Nokummus wrapped a deerskin rug around the girl's shoulders and settled down across from her, the low-burning fire between them. A fringe of flame sent quick flickers of shadow along the curved walls.

Nokummus had stopped the droning and was now drumming the fingers of one hand on her knee. She cleared her throat three or four times, and after each unnerving rasp, Addie was certain she was about to begin her story. But a long, uninterrupted silence followed, during which Addie bit down on her tongue to keep from complaining.

She was startled when Nokummus suddenly blurted out, "The man who loved the young woman wanted to take her away."

*Why not?* thought Addie. Isn't that the way love stories were supposed to go? But Nokummus didn't seem at all happy about it.

"The people said this will be a great loss to the tribe. They said the girl must stay and fulfill her destiny."

"How did they know what her destiny was?"

"A special Wampanoag ceremony can show the future. It can show the great beyond."

"Great beyond?"

"Destiny," said Nokummus.

*Another one of those riddles,* thought Addie. She didn't much like them.

"The girl must also stay to oversee the land passed down from her mother's mother's mother to her mother's mother to her mother."

Addie put a hand over her mouth to keep from giggling. She suspected that Nokummus must be speaking of tribal laws of inheritance, a serious issue that shouldn't be laughed at. She was surprised to think that Wampanoag land was passed down from woman to woman instead of man to man, that women were so important in the tribe. Yet Nokummus had said before that the young woman in the story had been thought of as a possible *pauwau*. The way she said it, Addie wondered if it was something like a queen.

"On the day before the tribal council was to meet, the young woman and man went before the white man's god. They married in secret and stole away. They received no tribal blessings, no gifts for prosperity and long life." Her eyes grew misty again, and she wiped them with her sleeve. "One day great preparations are being considered and plans made; the next day the entire tribe is mourning for a lost daughter."

*Daughter of the tribe,* thought Addie. Nokummus couldn't have meant her own daughter, but because of her great distress, Addie ventured to ask. "Was she — was she your daughter?"

"My only daughter," said the old woman.

"Were there no sons?"

"Two sons. But only one daughter. My daughter was named White Moon because of the soft light she cast over each day."

"But she came back?"

Nokummus's eyes filled up again. She seemed unable to continue, but at last she uttered just one word, "No."

"Why?" asked Addie. By the tremor of Nokummus's mouth and the way she closed her eyes tightly as if to move more deeply into herself, Addie knew it had been the wrong question. She didn't expect an answer and was surprised when her restive elderly companion, eyes still closed, spoke again.

"My daughter died in childbirth in the ancestral land of the Agawam."

"Didn't you go to her?"

"No one sent for me. I did not know she carried a child. I did not know where to find her." Her eyes roamed the windowless space. Large tears became trapped in the ridges of her brown cheeks. "After some time, I walked here to search for her, to find my daughter's husband, who builds boats, and plead with him to bring her back to Chappiquiddic."

"And did you find him? The man who builds boats? Did you find him?"

This person Nokummus spoke about was beginning to seem like a mythical figure; the story was starting to sound like the ones she'd told earlier about the Little People who vanished into thin air. But then she said, "It took many moons, but, yes, I did find him."

"Who was he? What was his name?"

Addie knew almost everyone around the town of Essex. She didn't remember a young Indian woman. People would have talked about it. There would have been a lot of gossip. Maybe Nokummus had the wrong town. Having often played among the headstones in the cemetery by the school, she knew all the engraved names. There were no recent Indian graves in it. Probably no Indian graves at all, even on the outskirts. Maybe the old woman had the wrong man.

"I never forgot his name," said Nokummus. "I never forgot the man who befriended my people and then stole my child."

"What was he called?"

"He is called Emerson Hayden," said Nokummus. "He is the same tall man you call Father."

The shock Addie felt at such a bizarre revelation was immediately followed by the thought that what Nokummus was saying didn't make any sense. She was angry that the old woman would implicate her papa in such an outrageous story. He had been head of another family — her family. He had been married to her mother, who had recently died. When was all this other life supposed to have happened? What had become of the half-breed baby?

"That's a crazy story," she said. "It isn't possible."

Oddly, Nokummus didn't answer but began to sing. It was a soft, simple tune the young girl had heard her sing before. Each time it filled her with such longing that she'd felt bereft when it ended. This time Nokummus repeated the tune over and over, clapping her hands all around as if in a game with children. Addie felt the clapping in her own still fingers, somehow knew the movements that were to come next, and entered mindlessly into the rhythms.

"Remember?" asked Nokummus with a sudden wide smile. She took Addie's hands in her own, and they clapped together as Addie searched for reasons why her very bones knew this child's play, why the tune entered her blood.

Nokummus stopped abruptly to reach to the back of the *wetu*, where she opened the top of a large covered basket. She took hold of Addie's hands again and put what she had retrieved into each of them—a grayish-white feather in one and a shiny quahog shell with deep violet edges in the other.

"Your birth feather and birth shell," she said solemnly, "given to you by your Wampanoag mother as she lay dying."

Dazed, Addie stared at the mundane objects. Such a common shell. Such an innocuous-looking feather. What meaning could they possibly hold for her?

"You're wrong, old woman," she said. "This story you've told me. It's all wrong. My real mother died in my arms. She rests in a pine box with my brother."

Addie was shaking now with rage and confusion. Although she couldn't remember what words Nokummus had used to lure her here or how the message had been transmitted, she began to berate her. "You promised to tell me the truth of things. What you've told is another story. It's only a story."

"It is your story," said Nokummus gently. "It is the story I must tell. Remember?" she repeated, reaching for Addie's hand again and softly touching the girl's forehead.

Addie pulled away and went to the other side of the *wetu*.

She refused to look up as Nokummus continued to speak to her.

"Remember trips into the forest when you were still carried in my arms? The long days when, as a child with no mother, I cared for you?"

This couldn't have happened. What she was saying. It couldn't be true.

"Your father had to work. And so I came to help. But then he found another wife and told me to go back to my tribe."

"Look," she said suddenly, crossing the *wetu* and placing an old arm against one of Addie's. "The skin is not as dark, but it's the same color." She raised a strand of Addie's hair. "And this. The color of a raven's wing."

"Papa had dark hair."

"Dark hair. Not black. Blue eyes."

His laughing eyes, transparent as seawater, and his kind face appeared to Addie more clearly than at any time since he'd left. They gazed at her fondly. "Where are you?" she wanted to ask the apparition before it disappeared. "I need you to tell me the truth of things. To tell me what really happened." But thinking of her own lie, the one she had carefully planned, written down, and almost sent all the way to the goldfields, she wondered if she even had a right to know.

# twenty

IN THE BITING AIR OF A WINTER DAWN, Addie slipped from the *wetu*. She could hear Nokummus's rumbling snores all the way to the outcropping of rock that jutted over the bay side of the river. A newly launched three-masted schooner, like a ghost ship framed against a gray sky, was making its way to open ocean, one white mainsail unfurled. Such vessels passed at all times of day with great regularity, and she wondered how many of them were on their way to the goldfields and which ones were bound for places she couldn't even imagine.

Gulls scattered as she approached. How she wished they hadn't flown from her. Oddly, this regretful feeling made her think again of Nokummus's story, of the song that had seeped through Addie like something that had once belonged to her, of the curiously close bond she'd immediately formed with the old woman. When she thought of these things, it seemed almost possible that Nokummus was telling the truth. "People of the morning light" Nokummus had called the Wampanoag more than once. As Addie repeated the phrase aloud, it resonated through her like the sun's warmth.

A loud noise as if something had fallen made Addie rush to check the squash gourd in which she planned to collect water from the Choate well. But since it was still balancing on the rock where she'd left it, she decided that one of the many deer on the island had probably sensed a human about and crashed into something as it gamboled away. She had just brushed off a cold, flat perch for herself when there was a loud rustling sound, and she looked back into the trees to catch any movement there. Shortly afterward, a very distinctive whistle made her jump up, and she was soon standing in the clearing above the rocks with her hands on her hips and her feet planted firmly on the frozen earth.

"John Tower," she yelled into the wind. "I know you're out there somewhere."

The whistling continued, but she couldn't decide where it was coming from. Whenever she thought she'd identified the direction, it would change — sometimes coming from behind, sometimes in front, sometimes from someplace over her head. She started turning in circles to find the perpetrator but only made herself dizzy. Disgusted with the trick, she grabbed the squash gourd and headed for the well. Halfway there, John sidled up next to her.

"I knew it was you I saw," he said, punching her shoulder. "When I was running Little Star on the beach in Ipswich, I looked over here and saw people on the island, and I knew it was you and that Injun. Clive said he thought so, too."

"If you were so sure, what made you row over?"

"What I don't know is why you want to live out here in some wigwam when there's people in town would take you in."

Another thing he didn't know, thought Addie, was that she had begun wondering the same thing, and that as time went on, her reasons for being here were becoming more and more complicated. Her thirteenth birthday had passed in January, but out here she'd had no inkling of what day it fell on, just as she hadn't known when the month itself had ended. Her mother had always baked a cake, and Papa would buy her at least one present. There was never any talk about the event of Addie's birth in the way there was of Jack's, and she'd been given to believe the experience had been an especially painful one, the kind that ladies didn't like to speak about except to one another.

"Just look at you," he said, stepping back for a better view. "At the way you're dressed. Like an Injun yourself. Where'd you get the deerskin britches?"

"Nokummus made them."

"Do you think she'd make a pair for me?"

"No. I don't know. I don't think so."

"Because I'm not an Injun. And you are. Right?"

Addie was stunned.

"Clive's been saying it's so," continued John, "but I told him he was off his nut. Now I'm not so sure."

*That makes two of us*, she thought. But how would Clive know? And if he did, was that why he'd always hated her? Maybe John had heard some other gossip. Maybe she should tell him how confused she was herself.

But instead she said, "My pa isn't Indian, and neither was my mother. You knew them both."

John shook his head and rubbed one ear. "That's true enough. And that's your pa's nose on your face, clear as day." He tweaked it and laughed.

"Then what are you going on about?"

"It's just," said John, "there's people say . . . well . . . They say your pa was married once before."

"What people?"

"Fellas in the yards. It's what they said when you went missing and we couldn't figure where to look."

Her head was heavy with all the information she'd suddenly been forced to assimilate. She was full of sparring emotions, conflicted thoughts and feelings. She wanted John to leave. She wanted him to stay. She wanted to leave with him. She wanted him to tell her everything would be all right. Torn as she was between the two worlds she seemed to inhabit, however, she knew she hadn't finished the search she'd begun months before. There were too many questions left unanswered. Too many things unresolved. And, she reminded herself, Nokummus had not yet found whatever she was looking for.

"It'll be spring soon," she said, not knowing where this sudden optimism was coming from. "Life on the island will be easier in the spring."

"And still make no sense. Guess I'll have to take Fanny to the Valentine's Day ice-cream social. Guess you'll still be out here waiting for a powwow or something."

The twinge of envy he'd obviously intended made her cheeks rosy. She turned away. Her voice grew small and ingratiating. "If you come again . . ." she began.

"Why would I?" He kicked a mound of icy snow with his boot.

"Well, if you do for one reason or another come again, would you bring my schoolbooks? I know it's a lot to ask, but I don't aim to get too far behind. There's firelight to read by and lots of time." Time had been hanging heavy lately. Often she felt so restless, she wanted to run shrieking up and down the drumlin. But since she wasn't ready to return to Essex and a life with strangers, she felt compelled again to swear John to secrecy.

"Promise," she said as she clasped a hand around his forearm and pulled a little to keep him still.

"Only if you promise that you are coming back . . . sometime," he said with a thin lift of hope in his voice.

"I am. I am coming back," she said. But she had no idea when that day would be or how long she would stay.

# twenty-one

IT WAS DAYS before Nokummus referred to the story she had told Addie about her supposed Indian mother. The girl had begun to wonder if she was ever going to bring it up again when the old woman came into the *wetu* with a basket full of ordinary tree bark from several different trees and squatted beside her. Thinking the bark was meant to help mend the birch flap torn by the wind in the storm just past, Addie asked if she could help.

"It is not for mending," said Nokummus. "It is for a special rite for Wampanoag girls and boys." She then described how the rite was only administered to those young people in the tribe who demonstrated the promise of special powers. She told how the dreams and hallucinations produced by a meal of bark and the vomiting that had to be endured after it would confirm Addie's bloodline and ancestry. "This ceremony," Nokummus said, "will tell if a girl has the strength and spirit to become a *pauwau*, a true leader, or if the boy can be a *pniese*, or warrior."

"What special powers have *I* demonstrated?" asked Addie. She knew it was futile to claim again that Nokummus was wrong about her birth mother. But she had no intention of agreeing to this peculiar ceremony, which sounded unbelievably awful.

"The time in the empty shipyard. The weeks you survived by your wits alone, as only a strong-willed and brave young woman, a leader of others, could do."

"You mean the time you forgot all about me?" Addie whispered to herself in a voice she thought Nokummus couldn't hear.

"I did not forget you. Not for one minute did I forget you. It was a test that every Wampanoag child of great promise must face, must conquer. My own daughter faced such a test."

Addie noted that she hadn't said, "Your own mother," even though she must be thinking it. She was about to tell Nokummus that she was definitely not going to eat that mess of bark in the basket when the old woman leaned closer to her and began what sounded like another story. Her breath came fast, as if she'd been trudging up a hill.

"If, after much retching and then a deep sleep, you are proven ready, Hobbamock will visit you in a dream. He will converse with you and make a pact of protection."

Forgetting that she didn't intend to eat the bark and have hallucinations, Addie asked, "Who is Hobbamock, and what will he protect me from?"

"Hobbamock is what we call the Warrior Spirit. He is the chief of warriors. If you show you do not fear him, he will protect you from all who mean to harm you."

"He didn't protect your daughter. She ran away and died." It was an unkind thing to say, but Addie was looking for any and all ways out of taking part in this strange rite, which was sounding more terrible by the minute.

I just won't do it, she said to herself as Nokummus ignored her cruel remark and continued talking about choosing the right season, the right phase of the moon, the right time after the onset of the first flow of menstrual blood. She said there was power in this important life change, and that now it had occurred, Addie's spirit was stronger than it would ever be.

Frightened and confused by this newest knowledge, Addie bit the tips of her fingers and curled up on her pallet like the child she still felt herself to be.

"On the land of our ancestors, there is a large *Pau Wau*, an important Wampanoag gathering to celebrate the bark ceremony, where all attend. Some night of the Snow Moon, we will make a small *Pau Wau*. We'll call animals to witness — *ottucke, whauksis, shannucke, ausupp*." The monotone in which she said the names sounded to Addie like a dirge. She wondered if her list included the foxes, the deer, the funny thin-tailed squirrels that overran the island.

"Not this night," said Addie. Not *any night*, she thought silently.

"We must make preparation," said Nokummus. She looked at Addie the way her mother used to when measuring her for a dress. "You must wear special clothing."

"And eat a special meal?" She was willing to go that far.

"No meal at all," said Nokummus. "You must fast for two entire days."

"Two days!" Addie exclaimed. She had hunger pains at just the thought of such an unreasonable deprivation. A soup of pheasant and roots had been simmering over the fire all afternoon. Surely the old one wasn't going to eat it all.

But Nokummus was rummaging through baskets as if Addie hadn't spoken and plans for the ceremony had already begun. After much quiet chortling to herself, she emerged with something folded across one arm, and she raised it reverently with both hands for Addie to see.

Still prone, Addie looked up from under an arm thrown over her head. "It's a beautiful dress," she finally acknowledged.

It was made of fringed deerskin, bleached almost white, and covered with an intricate pattern of beadwork depicting birds and animals. The little Addie knew of such handiwork, she was certain it had taken its creator many months to complete.

Nokummus smiled and held the garment close to herself as if in an embrace.

"This was the task of White Moon. This was the task she had to complete before the rite of bark."

Addie jumped up. "I haven't completed a task. I haven't made a dress or anything. We need to wait."

"No," said Nokummus. "You will wear the dress your mother made." She brought out heavily beaded moccasins stained with red and yellow ocher. "You will wear your own mother's moccasins."

"What's the hurry?" asked Addie.

"It is time," Nokummus said. "There is only so much time. We cannot wait for help from the tribe."

# twenty-two

LATER THAT DAY, Addie was still wondering why Nokummus felt the ceremony had to happen right away and what she had meant by "only so much time." Was she planning to leave soon? Had she intuited some natural disaster for which they should brace themselves? But the old woman had spoken with such authority and something so close to anger, her hands clenching the elaborate dress as she spoke, that Addie kept her questions to herself. She did, however, bring her bowl to the cooking pot when Nokummus began to fill her own.

"Today you begin your fast," said Nokummus as she pushed Addie's bowl away. Her eyes looked sympathetic enough, so Addie tried again.

On this second attempt, the old one took the bowl and held it tightly.

"You must grow hungry," she said. "You must endure it like a woman. Like your own mother."

"Own mother," Addie said with contempt. "My real mother would not make me starve."

She pulled her shawl around her and ran from the *wetu*, tears of rage stinging her eyes.

"And how will you know who is your real mother without this ceremony?" Nokummus called after her.

The old woman's words reached Addie as she paced outside in the night, and they hung in the frigid air like icicles. In moonlight, the river spun a shiny path just below, reminding her of how connected she still was to the mainland, how easily she could find her way back if she wanted to leave. But did she want to? Though she badly missed the day-to-day rituals of her former home life and the nearness of John and her pa, she had not yet learned what she'd come here for. She'd found only partial answers to all her searing questions of who she really was, of why she felt so different and restless, the questions that had ultimately driven her away from the townspeople of Essex and to this remote island with someone that most folks treated as an outcast. There were things about herself she still needed to understand. Maybe this strange rite, however repulsive to her, was one way to do that.

There had been nothing about such rites in the Bible stories Papa read to her. What kind of god did Nokummus worship?

She had trusted the old woman so completely before. What had happened to that trust? And although Addie felt forced by circumstance and her own convictions to make a life for herself here, she wondered how much longer she would need to be away from the things she knew and those people whom she held most dear.

Hungry and still conflicted, she knew there were no high-bush cranberries on the island and that she wasn't apt to find any other edible plants in this darkened landscape. She walked in circles around the *wetu* and then up to the Choate well, where a snowy owl sat like a pale observer on a low branch of one of the elms. Its yellow eyes and muted rumble of alarm seemed like something from the spirit world Nokummus insisted that she enter, and it sent her running down the slope. She had seen two or three of these creatures on her winter journey, always positioned in low places like silent messengers.

As she stood shivering before the *wetu* with both fear and cold, she watched smoke escape from the top of the enclosure and imagined the warmth inside. But she was too proud to reenter while the old woman was awake and waited in the bitter weather until she could hear the snores and wheezes that signaled she had fallen asleep. When Addie finally crept inside to slip under her deerskin rug and nurse her hunger, Nokummus was facing away from her with Matilda curled into the curve of her body as if the cat were choosing sides.

Even all by herself in the empty shipyard, she had not felt so alone. At that time, there was always the hope that the mysterious Indian woman would come and rescue her and tell Addie the secrets about herself she longed to know. If Nokummus were now going to pull away from her like this, Addie would never know for certain if White Moon was in fact the one from whom she'd received her deep connection to the earth and its creatures.

In the morning, Addie's stomach felt airy and calm as if feeding on a secret source. The pangs of the night before had passed, and she was resigned in a way she hadn't expected. When Nokummus, taciturn as the owls, handed her a bowl of water, she was suddenly aware of her great thirst and gulped it down. Throughout the day, the old woman kept her silence and ate her own regular meals, but gave Addie only water or broth. The girl didn't beg or wheedle for more, but went about her tasks and slept. Nokummus seemed neither surprised nor pleased, but treated her with an indifference that made Addie feel helpless. Not conscious of coming to a decision of any kind, she simply drifted through the hours and stayed out of the way.

Another day passed in much the same way, and Nokummus still didn't speak. By then Addie was feeling listless and resigned, but the stomach pains had returned until it felt as if a mouse were nibbling on the lining of her stomach. *I'll die this way,* she thought as she doubled over on her pallet. *She is starving me to death.*

To add insult, the *wetu* was awash in the sweet odors of Nokummus's meal of squash soup and dried rabbit meat. Addie listened to her companion chew each bite and slurp every spoonful. After the old woman had cleaned her bowl and put the scraps out for the deer, she sat down by the fire. Her breath came in ragged bursts as she struggled to settle herself.

"Tonight," came the voice Addie hadn't heard for two days. It was thick with disuse. "Tonight you will eat the meal of bark. You will eat it and dream."

# twenty-three

THE FIRST BITE WAS PINE-SCENTED and tasted woodsy, and Addie wondered why she'd feared it so. If it would please this woman who had helped her, it seemed a small price to pay, and there was the off chance she might truly learn something about herself, as Nokummus had promised. That was before she found how difficult the mixture was to chew and swallow. It scratched her throat, lodged in her chest, and made her choke.

"That's enough," she said when the mouthful had painfully passed into her system.

"Not enough," said Nokummus. She ground the bark more finely with her pestle and put a second spoonful to Addie's lips. The girl took it warily, washing it down with broth from the peculiar mix. Twice more her vigilant guide all but force-fed

Addie the terrible brew while she sputtered, tried to hold her mouth tightly shut, then put her hands in front of her face and cried, "No more."

As Addie sat back and caught her breath, Nokummus began to study her with a look so intense it bore like an arrow. She smoothed the ancestral dress that the girl wore, pulling it down in an attempt to cover the bare ankles of the child who had the bone structure of Emerson Hayden and whose large feet were pinched by the elaborate fur-lined moccasins.

The strangling sensation Addie began to feel in her chest was more violent than any hunger pains of the days just past. But Nokummus apparently didn't see the results she was looking for and continued urging her to consume more of the awful stuff in a power match that escalated until Addie was in such agony she thought she'd pass out.

"I can't! I can't!" she screamed at last while she clutched her throat and gagged.

Almost instantly her convulsing body lurched out the door of the *wetu* and into a snowbank, where she vomited over and over and over until she brought up water and a little blood. This was followed by dry heaving that produced nothing at all. Gasping for air, she collapsed facedown by the putrid steaming mess just before the world began to spin uncontrollably and she lost any conscious hold.

At first, utter blackness, then it was as if the wings of an eagle were trying to sprout on the leaden body of the dead. It was painful, this metamorphosis from arms to wings, and Addie fought the strange feelings and the yeasty way the wings continued to form and rise until they spread out from her shoulders like giant iridescent fans. Not certain how she would be able to lift them and set them in motion, she was suddenly climbing into the sky and being swept through sun-filled air troughs or carried effortlessly on downdrafts and strong currents. Campfires burned below her night flight; war whoops and drumbeats rose over the mountains and plains, through the trees, and into her avian blood.

Later, she remembered everything less in detail than in broad sweeps of sense and feeling — the smell of a thousand forests, the rush of many rivers. A fierce dawn propelled her anima into that of an elk, and she felt the rush of air across her haunches as she leaped through northern woods on small round hooves. Swiftly transformed once again, she was a goat clinging to the side of a mountain, the taste of grass in her mouth. When she found herself in the den of the cougar, the dank odors were as repellent to her as his dark heart, a place that she made no attempt to enter. But she was one with the power of him, the sinewy strength, and, in what seemed like an entire season, she hunted and prowled.

Swept at length into the eye of the wind, she could feel herself being broadcast upon the earth in fragments as tiny as the beams of the moon. At times she seemed to have disintegrated; at others she was lost in a spirit sea filled with all creatures from the beginning of the world. Often her passage through this vast dream landscape appeared swift; sometimes it was not contained by time at all. For a great measureless span, she floated in a warm salt sea, barely aware, barely moving. Mostly, she was at peace within the watery confines; sometimes she stretched out a hand or foot and felt a spongy resistance.

At length, a terrible restlessness consumed whatever she had become, and she knew that something momentous was about to happen. In what seemed like only minutes, the sea erupted and the waters eased her through a dark passage into a place of blinding light, light that seeped through the membrane of her tightly shut lids. She could feel large hands upon her head, then along her small body. She was lifted and wrapped and held. A piercing cry she could not control seemed to delight whatever shadowy creatures were around her. A woman was speaking softly, with unbelievable warmth. Held against this woman, Addie was lulled by the faint comforting tune of a song she was certain she had always known. It had completely filled her blood and entered her soul before the dream ended in the same way it had begun, with interminable darkness.

It took a number of hard shakes and Nokummus's loudest voice to bring Addie reluctantly back to the present, where she slowly found herself again in the *wetu*, weak with sweat under her deerskin, the song still traveling through her head and heart.

"You have slept two days," said the old one. Though she appeared to be separated from Addie by a thick haze, the girl could sense her concern. The woman removed the ceremonial dress, washed Addie with cool sea sponges, and dressed her in a clean garment of deerskin. Speechless and exhausted, Addie allowed herself to be cared for. She wanted to tell Nokummus something of her extraordinary passage through time, but there were no adequate words. Feeling helpless, she fell back into a dreamless sleep and didn't emerge from it until the smell of corn pudding teased her awake. When Nokummus handed her a full bowl, Addie ate the contents gratefully. The old woman did not prod her to tell of her vision quest until much later when she asked, "And Hobbamock. Did you have a meeting with Hobbamock?"

By then some parts of Addie's astonishing journey were growing fuzzy, but she was sure she would have recalled a meeting with the chief of warriors. It had been one of the things she'd desperately wanted to avoid. Apparently, she'd been successful.

"I don't think so," she told Nokummus, and the woman's face became so troubled that Addie considered making something up. Though some details had become indistinct, the experience itself still penetrated with a force that was indescribable. She wanted to tell Nokummus all about it. She wanted to say something that would explain exactly what she had learned. But the old woman appeared unwilling to let go of her foregone conclusions about Addie's dream and the belief that this was indeed the first step to the girl becoming the *pauwau* that Nokummus wanted her to be. To Addie, Nokummus's unwillingness to let go of her expectations was almost visible, much like an impenetrable aura or shield. She saw no way to dissuade her.

Addie reached for the feather in her basket, which she'd come to realize was from a snowy owl, spotted in places and yellowed with age. She held the quahog shell until it grew warm in her hand. This bivalve, Nokummus had explained, was as valuable to the Wampanoag as money. She cautiously placed them both in Nokummus's lap.

The old Indian looked up at her, her entire face a question. She was about to speak herself when Addie interrupted her and opened her arms.

# twenty-four

SHE WAS SURPRISED when Nokummus didn't rise to embrace her. In the firelight, the whites of the Indian's dark eyes glowed red; her leathery skin appeared glazed with gold, and her lips were pressed together in an expression of triumph. Addie noticed these things as she waited for some action, some affectionate word or touch from this person whom she had come to believe was possibly her closest relative besides her own father. She had done all the things Nokummus had asked of her; she had participated in the ceremony, endured the physical pain, taken the terrifying excursion of dreams. What more could the old woman possibly want? A true grandmother would have simply reached up to take her in her arms.

Not until Addie let her own arms grow limp did Nokummus rise.

"So. You are ready now, Little Red Tree?" she said, her voice almost a whisper, her mouth not a handbreadth away from Addie's ear. It was the first time the girl had heard what she guessed was her own Indian name, and though not receiving the caress she might have expected, it warmed her to hear these words spoken in Nokummus's voice. "You are ready to take the position in the tribe that White Moon shunned."

Addie hadn't expected such a leap from one thing to the next. Yes, she was certain now of her Wampanoag blood, but the thought of returning with Nokummus to the Chappiquiddic tribe confused and frightened her. Her home had always been here in Essex. When her father came back, it would again be with him. But how could she tell this to Nokummus, who was so obviously overjoyed?

"When Papa returns," she gently told the old woman. Her words were soft and reflective. "He will need me to keep house. My place will be here with him."

"If he returns," replied Nokummus gently in a way that made Addie realize her grandmother had never desired such an outcome but felt she needed to prepare Addie for such a possibility. "We will have to wait and see."

Addie had long ago explained to Nokummus the exact nature of his trip, and more than once the old woman had told her how there could be unimagined dangers during such a long and difficult journey. But Addie had never allowed herself to think he might not come back. Hearing Nokummus say it out loud like this didn't change her resolve.

The woman's words continued to jump ahead. "First, you must help me find the grave of your mother."

*So that is what you've been looking for*, thought Addie. She realized at once that she could probably do that, for her eyes were sharp and she now knew the island well. But since Nokummus had been searching for it a long time with no success, perhaps she'd been looking in the wrong place.

"Little Red Tree," Addie repeated slowly without addressing Nokummus's entreaty. "Why was I called that?"

"Your father said you were a very long baby, very red in the face. He said your mother bestowed the name, as is proper, before she died."

If her father knew this, why had she never heard the name before?

"And the feather and shell?"

"Chosen by your mother before you were born. Quahog for great worth. Snowy owl to protect a daughter of winter." She smiled. "Wise choices."

"And why do you think she was buried here? Here on Hog Island?"

"Your father said he gave her an Indian burial. I believe that such a burial is not allowed in the white man's graveyard. He said the grave can be found on an island."

"Didn't he tell you which one?"

"He said he didn't want you to know about your first mother. He didn't want you to someday know of the place of the grave."

Addie tried not to believe what Nokummus was saying. Pa was a kind man. A good father. But why hadn't he told Addie anything about what she now thought to be true? Or divulged the place of White Moon's grave to this old woman who mourned so for her daughter? Had she been purposely living in the area for such a long time just so she could find it?

"Like the snowy owl," Nokummus said as if in answer. "I stayed here to watch over you, too."

"What about your family? Your sons?"

"They are grown men with wives and children. Each has moved to his own wife's *wetu*."

Addie was transfixed by the enormity of what Nokummus was telling her. This woman had lived like a nomad for thirteen years, been deprived of the company and assistance of her family and tribe in order to find her daughter's grave and have brief glimpses of a half-white grandchild. The lady Addie had always called mother had never admitted the Indian woman into their house, had never spoken her name. Her father had purchased the clams and vegetables she sold as if she were a common peddler.

The intense feelings Addie was beginning to recognize were ones of shame. Shame that this old woman had been forced to live in such a way. Shame that there was some important part of herself that the people closest to her had wanted to keep secret.

Yet the woman who raised her, the one she had always called mother, had taken good care of her, and Addie still loved her. She loved her father with all her heart.

"How much did my pa love White Moon?" she asked.

"Enough to steal her from her ancestral home," Nokummus said with contempt. "To give her what he called a better life. What better life could there be than with her own tribe?"

Papa had made a good life in Essex. If White Moon was her true birth mother and she had survived, Addie was sure they would have all been happy together. But she was still trying to put all the parts of the story in place. What if White Moon had lived? What would have happened to Emmaline? What if there had never been her brother, Jack? It was a puzzle with so many pieces it made her dizzy. She took out the daguerreotype of the family she thought she knew and

167

tried to imagine a different face, a darker countenance in place of the one belonging to the person she realized now might have been her stepmother.

"Is there a photograph? A photograph of my mother?" she asked.

For an instant Nokummus seemed flustered. She passed a hand over her heart and then down her body to a leather pouch she kept at her waist. She opened it slowly and drew out a battered piece of heavy paper, creased in many places. One side was blank, but when she turned it over, sepia tones and lights and shadows were apparent. She handed it to Addie.

The photo was faded, and she had to smooth it flat to see the three figures depicted. One was an Indian boy in a breechcloth. Two were young women, very unlike each other but in traditional Wampanoag dress. One girl looked shyly at the ground. The one with a feather in her hair was looking directly at the camera. A familiar head of straight black hair cascaded from beneath the beaded band that held the feather, heavy tresses so like her own. The intensity of the eyes, even in such a small likeness, made Addie feel as if she were looking into a mirror. It wasn't her face exactly. Not really. But the energy it held, the curiosity in the eyes. The sense of these entered her like an unbroken life force and turned her silent with a deep feeling of sudden satisfaction. Of course this was her mother. There could be no doubt.

"The word *nokummus*," said Addie. "It means 'grandmother,' doesn't it? I've been calling you grandmother right along."

The old woman nodded, then bowed her head as if trying to hide her sly smile.

# twenty-five

IN THE COLDEST DAYS OF FEBRUARY, when food was especially scarce, Nokummus directed Addie to climb the part of the drumlin some distance from the *wetu* and uncover a storage pit set into a sandy place in the hill. The landmarks of twin rocks and a dead tree were clear, and she had no trouble discovering it, yet after she'd removed layers of stiff cattail mats, she was surprised at what she found—a deep pit lined with more cattail mats that held several bags of dried corn, beans, and nuts. She took a few bags from their resting place and re-covered the others.

On her way back, she noticed a red shape bobbing in the river and was trying to decide what it was and if it belonged there, when it lurched forward until all sides were visible and she could clearly see it was a dory. Its recent occupant was climbing toward her and waving something that he held in his hand.

"John," she exclaimed with unconcealed pleasure, more to herself than to him. She was amused at how he loped even when traveling uphill. He appeared to be taller than the time she'd last seen him and was just as ruddy-faced and determined.

"With the ice floes broken up some," he said when he grew closer, "I thought I'd bring you your heart's desire." He grabbed her about the waist with his free arm and danced her around in circles. "A letter from your pa."

She had almost stopped hoping for one. Pa was so far away after all, and no one but John knew where to find her. "How'd you get ahold of it?" she cried.

"Easy. Just told Mrs. Hardy I'd keep it for you. It's addressed to your ma, so she didn't know what else to do with it, anyway. I think the Astoria or the Sarah Franklin may have brought it back."

The envelope had no stamps at all, just like others she'd seen that had come through on returning ships. It was water-stained but dry now and tightly sealed. She held it in her hand awhile, almost afraid to look inside.

"Aren't you gonna open it?"

She jabbed a finger into a loose end and ripped through to what was inside. There were actually two smaller envelopes and two letters. The one to Addie and Jack was longer than she'd expected, but the words were inscribed in her father's careful and precise hand. She began reading it to herself, starting again out loud when she saw the curious look on John's face and the way his eyes turned up at the edges with expectancy.

Dear Ones:

I hope this finds you well. There has been little sickness on board the Metropolis, and God has granted us a smooth voyage.

We made Valparaiso yesterday noon. It is a very large and beautiful harbor filled with vessels from every nation. This splendid city rises from the water to the mountains. The streets are paved. Imagine. Everywhere are bright-colored houses. There are peaches and quinces in abundance and crawfish, a creature much like our lobster. Once ashore, you can ride a wagon anyplace for 12½ cents. A French frigate entered as we arrived and gave a salute of twenty-one guns. A stirring sight. It is a different world here altogether. I wonder, will San Francisco or Sacramento hold as many marvels?

I often think of you all together in our warm little house. Jack growing and learning. Addie reading and exploring. And your dear mother so quiet and lovely at her loom. It is a picture that serves to remind me of the reason for this long separation and the prize I seek that can only improve our lives.

Your loving Papa

Stunned by actually receiving the letters and by the wonder at what hers contained, Addie stared dry-eyed across the bay. Papa had traveled thousands of miles to reach such a place as he described; her new world had been only across the span of a familiar river. How she wished she could talk to him about it.

She didn't open the one marked *Emmaline*. What her father and stepmother had shared had been so private and polite. And whatever this second note contained, Addie knew it wasn't meant for her eyes. She would return it to him in its sealed envelope when he came home.

"I never did mail my letter," she confessed to John.

"And he doesn't know you're living like an Indian."

There was a hint of disdain in his voice, but she so badly wanted to tell him what she'd recently learned about herself that she chose to ignore it. The magnitude of her recent experiences still excited and confounded her, and she needed to share them. But he left her no opening and didn't even pause before passing on information of his own.

"I worked on the horn timber myself for the stern of this new vessel. Mabry told Mr. Loeb he reckoned I was ready, so they set me to work alone on it. It's an important job, Addie. One that's not just passed around to any fool shipwright."

She looked at his hands, capable hands, the size of a man's and calloused. She was sure he could master any job he wanted to learn. She knew without doubt that his future in the yards was secure and would become even more so. He had no conflict about who he was and what he should do. He was surrounded by brothers and sisters and had a living mother and father who farmed the land and stayed in one place. Could he possibly understand the ways in which she was torn? Would he feel differently about her if he knew?

"That's just wonderful, John," she said, and meant it. She held her heavy shawl close, the shawl she'd come to realize must have been made by her birth mother. The patterns of animals and birds were as colorful and distinct as those on the deerskin dress; it was so unlike any of the soft and pale items that Emmaline had woven for her.

"I knew you'd want to know," he said shyly. "I wanted you to have a notion why I haven't been to school much these past months."

She wondered why he was acting as if she'd disapprove.

"I mean, I know how important learning is to you and all. I don't want you or Miss Fitzgibbon to think any the less of me."

"I'm not your teacher, John," she said. "And how you want to live your life is up to you." The last were words she'd dearly like to hear from him, but they seemed to have a disquieting effect upon John, and she regretted saying them.

"Here," he said as he handed her a parcel of two books — the one on the China trade and her arithmetic primer. He'd even brought her a slate and some chalk. Except for the letter from her father, it had been so long since she'd read either letters or numbers, since she'd recited a poem or put down a cipher, that she felt as ignorant as a small child who'd never been to school. The books felt solid and right in her hands, and she couldn't wait to open their covers. So grateful for what he had brought her, she held them against her like fragile crockery and couldn't speak.

"You asked me to bring 'em. Remember?" said John. "You did want them?"

"Oh, yes, John," she all but squealed. "Oh, I do want them. I want them so badly." She would have kissed him if not for the consternation it would likely cause for both of them. Since childhood, they'd never so much as hugged each other. But she could see he was pleased at the effect of his gift, pleased and a little amused at how greatly she valued it.

"Do you ever aim to go back to school again?" he asked.

"Of course I do. I will. These books will help me catch up, so I won't be left behind."

"It's me whose being left behind. I'm just now learning how to build ships. The book learnin' will have to wait."

Nokummus was standing at the bottom of the drumlin, staring at John as if at a species of animal she'd never seen before. Even from this distance, Addie could tell the old woman wasn't happy. She wanted to invite John back to the *wetu* to get warm. She knew he'd be surprised at how comfortable it was. But would her grandmother allow it? As she was trying to decide what to do, John said, "I've got to go now, Addie. I'm supposed to be dubbing the *Spring Hill*, but I knew how much you've been wanting to hear from your pa."

"Little Star and Fleur?" she asked.

"It's been so long, I reckon they think they've found a home."

This made her sad at first, but then she was flooded with relief that they were not missing her the way that she missed them, the way she missed seeing John almost every day and relying on him. She was happy to find that he was still as kind as ever, still worried about her.

"When are you coming back?" he asked. "My ma will take you in for sure if you just say the word. She wasn't well enough before, and there's not much room, but we'd make do."

If he had asked earlier, if she had thought it was a possibility all those months ago, would she have chosen to stay? She could feel the answer opening within her like an early spring flower, perfect and complete. In spite of any hardships she'd had to endure, she was grateful to be here on this island and to know the truth of things at last. Grateful and apprehensive.

# *twenty-six*

ADDIE WATCHED FROM THE HILLTOP as John rowed away in the bright dory, each dip of the oar pulling him back to the world they both knew. She ached to return with him to that place, if just for a little while, to be nothing but an earnest, playful child again, eager to please her pa. As she pulled her glance away from John's receding figure, it fell on Nokummus, still standing at the bottom of the other side of the hill, still watching her with narrowed eyes and a distinct frown. When Addie began to slip and slide her way down the slope toward Nokummus, the old woman turned and walked into the *wetu* without a word.

It wasn't until evening that her grandmother mentioned anything about John's visit, and then her words were meager and her delivery of them curt. She had settled herself before the fire, her sewing in her lap, her eyes squinting at the close work, before she spoke.

"That boy desires a wife."

Addie struggled not to laugh, for she could see that Nokummus was in dead earnest. She took time to phrase a reply that wouldn't appear as flippant as the first thing that came to her mind.

At last she said, "John's my oldest friend. He's my school-mate, not my beau." *And I'm only thirteen,* she wanted to add, but Nokummus had told her that in the eyes of the tribe, she was now a woman on the brink of spiritual growth and a new identity. Did this old woman think John would steal her away as her father had once stolen White Moon?

"A friend can become a husband."

"Don't worry," said Addie, and reached out to touch her hand. As it quivered like a frightened sparrow, she felt compelled to repeat, "Please don't worry." What more could she say? How could she reassure this woman who had lost so much, and what, after all, was Addie willing to promise her?

Because of Nokummus's simmering anger at Addie's father, the girl decided to keep the letter and its contents to herself. Earlier, when she'd described Pa's journey to Nokummus, her grandmother had expressed disdain again of any search for gold that would take a man away from his family. In her mind, Addie reasoned, she must believe that she's rescuing the child that he'd forsaken for his own selfish interests. A number of times she'd mentioned, in a strange offhand way, that many accidents could happen in the goldfields, how the lives of some of the Argonauts, as these gold seekers called themselves, could so easily be lost at sea going to or coming from their destination. It was, it seemed to Addie, as if she didn't mean to be unkind but was preparing her for any eventuality.

The old woman would certainly not be happy to hear about Pa's adventures in the way that Addie was. And she truly was, for she'd long ago excused this trip as something for the family's common good, and she fully empathized with her father's love of exotic places and unexpected discoveries. The anger that she did feel, however, was more complicated and centered on the tangled truth of things she'd had to find out for herself. Why had she been left so in the dark? Why had Pa tried to wipe away his former life and any trace of Addie's true mother and rich heritage? There was no way she could answer this letter from out here on Hog Island, and, until she saw him face-to-face, no possible way she could ask the burning questions that haunted her.

Most of the following week, a parade of sea smoke marched up the river and obscured the colorless bay beyond. Too cold to venture far for days, Addie read from her arithmetic primer and worked with ciphers on her slate. She puzzled over the fractions she'd only begun to learn but quickly grasped the formula. The book on the China trade, which had failed to capture her interest during school hours, now seemed to contain a wealth of fascinating information. Addie was glad of the warmth that Matilda provided as she curved across her feet or stretched out in her lap.

From time to time, Nokummus would look over at the girl, so consumed by her studies, with a probing watchful gaze. The resolute old woman's story voice had returned, and Addie was happy to find that they could once again pass dark evenings with more tales of the Makiaweesug, magic animals, and someone called Elder Grandmother Spider, who was all-seeing and godlike.

The temperature rose during the first days of March, but in spite of the return of some migrating birds and the bursting of many hard buds on bushes and trees, fierce winds whipped the island both day and night. It wasn't until a surprisingly calm and clement day on which a few robins had appeared among the crows that Nokummus decided they should begin again to search for White Moon's grave. She and Addie had already discussed the possibility that it might in fact be on another, smaller island, and so they decided on Corn Island, the smallest one of all. Nokummus had once traveled there in milder weather to bring back clay. It was just below Hog and easy to get to in the canoe. If they found nothing there, they could later try Dilly Island or the much larger Cross.

Though there'd been a red sky in the east that morning, which usually warned of a storm, Nokummus, intent on this search, studied the air herself—breathing in, sniffing, and pressing it between open palms before finally deciding it was safe to proceed. Addie was sent to ready the canoe, but she didn't push it off the bank and into the water until she could actually see Nokummus meandering toward her with a large basket on one arm. The girl had no idea what it contained but noticed how protectively her grandmother held it against her hip, and so she didn't offer to help carry it. When the old one was firmly kneeling with her basket tucked against her, Addie gave the canoe a final push into the water and jumped in.

They each took a paddle, and though they were traveling against the current, it was a neap tide and the sleek hull whistled as it passed through the tips of the submerged grasses and over the inlets through Great Bank, making it appear as if their passage was swift. They could actually see Corn from their launching spot, so it took no more than fifteen minutes to arrive at a much smaller version of the island they had just left. You could, in fact, almost see over it to the water beyond. Addie had heard tales of how animals — sheep mostly — had once been raised out here, and there were stiles and broken fences to affirm what she'd been told. Almost as treeless as Hog Island, it seemed an unlikely grave site, and Nokummus must have thought so, too, for at first she refused to leave the canoe. But Addie believed that since they were here, they should at least look around. Aware that the old woman had been more inclined to follow her lead since the bark ceremony, she jumped out and began exploring. This time, it was quite a while, however, before Nokummus would agree to extricate herself and her basket and follow. With so few trees to break the wind, it was difficult to travel even a short distance, and she was full of uncharacteristic complaints. "There is no flat land." "There is too much wildness." "There is no place of rest."

As Addie trudged ahead through the brambles and over the rough, cold island, she began to agree with her. But in spite of the discomfort, the scattered sunlight made the pebbles glisten, and the air was fresh with the taste of salt. For some time she tramped back and forth and poked fruitlessly into every hillock and recessed place.

She was just about to give up when she came across a surprisingly bare stretch of ground near their landing place on the side closest to the mainland. Anyone would pause at such a space, protected from the elements by beach plum and sumac and clear of the surrounding briars and vines. A small piece of polished granite was placed at one end. The precise shape of the stone, the solitary way it was positioned, gave it dignity and defined it as something that had been put there by human hands.

She stooped to look more closely, and she saw that it was engraved with a thin crescent moon. Almost afraid to believe that this could possibly be the grave they were looking for, Addie didn't call to Nokummus right away or make any move to summon her. She did kneel and she did reach out instinctively to caress the ground with the flat of her hands as she tried to picture the mother she had never known. And she said a prayer to the God whom she'd been taught to believe in, the God whom, during this long winter, she'd begun to think belonged to everyone and answered to many names.

When Nokummus came upon her, the old woman silently bent down to run her fingers over the roughly engraved moon while her lips moved inaudibly in a supplication of her own. Her soft keening broke the quiet as she rocked back and forth on her heels. Addie rose and put her arms around the stooped figure to hold her still and share her grief, and soon each one's face was shiny with tears.

"Such a lonely place," her grandmother said at last, in a voice grown thin and shallow. "There were no drums for my daughter or cleansing ritual. No burial robes marked with soot. No way to know if her body was even sprinkled in red ocher and curled on its side in this last sleep." She sighed deeply and began to rummage in her large basket, pulling one thing out, then another, things that Addie had never seen before — some odd-colored glass bottles, a shiny metal pot, a clay pipe, a delicate string of shell beads. These she lay close to the piece of granite, pressing them deep into the sandy soil.

"But you said Papa told you he had observed the Wampanoag burial customs," said Addie to console her.

"Yes. Your papa told me that," Nokummus countered dismissively, "but how can I be sure?" Then she continued to lament. "She is so far away from the tribe. She is so all alone." And she crooned to herself, "All these years, all these years," over and over as if to punctuate her deep regret for not finding the grave site sooner.

Only much later — when the chill wind had begun to numb Addie's fingers and nose, and the yellowing sky became swollen with purple clouds — did she interrupt the old woman's deep reverie and lead her back to the canoe.

As she pushed it into the river, a streak of lightning cracked so close it raised the hair on her arms and head. A deafening peal of thunder broke just an instant later, and Addie wished they'd paid attention to the red-sky warning. It looked now as if they'd be caught in a squall unless they could make it back before the clouds opened up and swamped the dugout. She looked straight ahead to the northwest and paddled as fast as she could, keeping her eyes on the shoreline just below their little settlement, where something seemed to be moving. Maybe Matilda was chasing the gulls again. But on coming closer, she noticed a small skiff and a figure running toward it along the narrow beach. The gangly person all but flew into the boat, his cap sailing from his head. As the skiff pulled away, a sudden ruff of fire appeared at the base of the *wetu*, and before they'd traveled even the additional length of a schooner's hull, flames were licking the birch-bark walls and leaping into the air.

There was a sharp thunderclap, a swift darkening of the sky, and great sheets of water began to pour over them as if from a giant bucket. Addie had never been so wet, so frightened, so angry, or so helpless. In the melee of water and wind, and with the inertia of Nokummus's dragging paddle, she couldn't even seem to move the craft forward, and she was crying tears of frustration the entire interminable way back to the shore. When they finally reached it, she ran to the *wetu*, which was now steaming under the same downpour that had drenched her and her grandmother. The scene smelled of burned trees, charred animal skins, and wet ash.

Hot embers were still glowing a threatening red under what remained of the sputtering, spitting blaze.

Nokummus came up behind Addie and dropped her paddle. She stood motionless and her gaze was frozen, even as her sudden cry of anguish carried across the river they had just crossed. Smoke and distance were already obscuring the person in the skiff heading for the mainland, but Addie's gut told her who it was—who it had to be. Clive Ogilvy. The same boy who had killed her rooster, the one who had tormented her since her first day of school, and whose soggy but familiar woolen watch cap was now swishing in and out with the ripples. John had said that Clive knew she was living on Hog Island, and now that bully had come here and destroyed their home.

"Hobbamock," Nokummus hissed through her teeth, when she seemed able to speak at all, "Hobbamock is sending a message."

"No," Addie said. "The one who did this isn't a great warrior but more like some kind of devil. His name is Clive."

"I never heard of a Clive devil. It must be Hobbamock. He is displeased with you."

"With me?" What had she done now? What could she possibly have done for her grandmother to think she deserved such a terrible punishment? Half of the *wetu* was destroyed; many of their belongings had been turned to ash. She picked up her mother's ceremonial dress. It smelled of smoke but was still intact. Most of the clay pots were black; Nokummus's bed was a pile of burned rubble, her eel spear and dip net and other implements a heap of cinders.

And now Addie was being told by this person she had come to love and depend upon that Addie herself was responsible.

# *twenty-seven*

SHIVERING AND SOGGY, they dragged themselves all the way to the Choate property, carrying as much as they could fit into Nokummus's large empty basket. Addie hauled an armload of any clothing that might still be usable as well as her haversack, which had escaped unharmed along with the treasures it contained — the daguerreotype of her family, the feather and shell, John's father's watch, which she'd stopped winding long ago, and the two letters from her pa. The deer-skins were, for the most part, charred beyond reclaim; any still usable pottery was too bulky to take with them wher-ever they might be going; Addie's books had been destroyed. For the present, they hoped to find shelter in the Choate barn, but even as she pried loose the heavy board that held the doors and flung them open, Addie was overcome by the pervading chill of the empty, cavernous place and knew they could never get warm here.

"Matilda. Matilda," she called out every little while, shaking her head and brushing back tears when there was no answer. They had looked all around for the independent cat at the site of the burned *wetu*, but to no avail. Forced to move on by Nokummus's weakened condition, Addie could only hope that her pet had simply gone into hiding at the sight of the fire and would soon emerge to follow them the way she had trailed Addie all those miles to the empty shipyard.

Adjacent to the Choate property was a farm where a man named William Marshall made cheese that he sold in the Essex markets. They had seen him off and on during the winter months as he brought corn fodder, straw, and meadow hay to the little herd of cows that he kept in a small barn. She'd observed that sometimes he came over from the mainland for the day or stayed awhile in the tiny adjacent farmhouse, and the cows were let out to the barren pasture. For the many weeks just past, the cows were seldom out, and Addie suspected they were drying off until spring and producing little milk. She recalled again how the man had passed her once or twice on the main path but never so much as nodded.

By the time Addie and Nokummus reached the Marshall barn, the old woman was shaking badly and walking so slowly, the girl knew she'd have to get her out of the elements as soon as possible. Inside, the breath and wind of the animals and the smell of manure were almost overpowering, but there was body heat and there were extra blankets unused by the heifers. When it was nearly dusk, knowing the light would soon fail, Addie and Nokummus removed their wet clothing and hung it from any pegs or rafters to dry. In the shadowy gloom of the barn, the thin naked body of her grandmother seemed so feeble, so vulnerable, that the sight filled Addie with an unexpected tenderness and made her more determined than ever to protect this aged woman who had come to mean so much to her. Addie wrapped herself and Nokummus in the stiff and reeking blankets and found a warm place between the cows. She added clean straw from the hayloft and made a bed as best she could for her grandmother, who appeared exhausted and confused as she stumbled over to it.

The girl lowered herself beside her and held her close, and as they lay there in the dark with a soft wind whispering through the eaves, little by little, the violent shivering began to subside. Outside, the storm had passed as quickly as it had come, but Addie continued to worry about Matilda. How could the cat find them here in this barn? Would she think she'd been left behind?

In her sleep, the old woman's breathing was shallow and uneven. The cows had thrashed and mooed all night long.

Both these disturbances had caused Addie to sleep fitfully and to be grateful for the warmer March air that filtered through cracks in the barn. The thought of Hobbamock and his displeasure added to her sleeplessness. How could her grandmother think such a thing! She racked her brain for the reason.

By morning, Nokummus's breathing was less ragged. Addie was still curled against her warm body, wide awake but strangely peaceful. Her eyes had been open for some time before she caught the glimmer of a large spiderweb in one corner of the stall. It hung like a semicircle of fine lace, each thread appearing to be spun from the silvery morning light that crept through a crack in the wall. Awed by its intricacy of design and the way it wavered with anything as slight as the breath of a heifer, she couldn't take her gaze away. How could anything so fragile be so strong? The question itself and the mysterious answer that she was trying to grasp made her somehow less afraid of what lay ahead. She had survived thus far partly by her own wits. Nokummus, too, weak as she'd appeared of late, had drawn in the past from a reservoir of strength that was largely invisible. *Spider Grandmother*, thought Addie, remembering the godlike figure of the Wampanoag. Like the spider, she and Nokummus were weaving their destiny out of threads both luminous and strong.

With the growing light of day came the pervading thought that Mr. Marshall might come by to milk or water the cattle. But after the earliest hours had passed and there was no sign of him, Addie pulled her damp clothing from the railings and pegs, dressed herself, and gathered some feed from the bin beside the door to fill the feeding troughs. The sleepy-eyed cows ignored her efforts and sank farther into the hay, unwilling to exert themselves.

Nokummus didn't stir until much later. When she did, an initial look of confusion was soon replaced by one of panic. Hunched over in the straw, she pulled the cow's blanket more tightly around her bare body and droned her grief and fear.

When the wailing had subsided, she said, "We must leave before the farmer comes."

"I don't think he's apt to be by," said Addie. It looked as if the cows had not been milked for a while, but their udders weren't swollen.

"But we can't stay here," said Nokummus, and Addie had to agree. Even though the weather was mild today, March was an unpredictable month that could easily produce another snowstorm. They needed to find something more perma-nent and out of the weather, and Mr. Marshall was bound to return very soon. The way he had totally ignored their presence on the island convinced Addie that they would not be welcome here.

"There is nothing on this island to build a new *wetu* with," Nokummus grumbled. Addie thought back to the story of how her grandmother had brought the saplings, the birch bark, the cattail mats all the way from the mainland in her dugout. She had been so strong then, even when telling about it. She had seemed so in command. What had happened to that strength and resolve?

Addie had absolutely no desire to try to figure things out on her own and be the one in charge. She desperately wanted to turn any decisions about where they should go over to Nokummus, telling herself that maybe in a day or two her grandmother would feel stronger and could resume that role.

They hadn't eaten since the morning of the day just past, and Addie knew that food was the first thing she had to find. Even though there were more bags of corn and beans still buried in the hillside, where could they build a fire and what could they cook in? She left the barn to see if the farmer's house was open, but the only door was locked tight. On her way there, however, she'd passed through a small, clean anteroom. It was lined with shelves that still held a few wheels of cheese from another season. She thought of how they must have been frozen through the winter and thawed in this milder weather and might easily be spoiled. But since it was the only food she could scurry up in a hurry, she took the cheesecloth off the top of one and dug out chunks of the white cheese with her bare hands. It was pungent and strong and a little tough, but not so affected by its long storage as to be inedible. And it quickly quieted the gnawing sensation in her stomach. She hoped it would do the same for Nokummus but was prepared to have her refuse anything so foreign to her diet of roots and wild things. The old woman did indeed have little appetite for it, but like an obedient child, she took a few mouthfuls before falling back against the side of a reclining cow that mooed amiably and didn't budge.

The water gourd was still usable, and Addie filled it from the pump outside the barn. She bent down to place the container against Nokummus's dry lips, took some swallows of her own, and then refilled the gourd to take with them on whatever journey lay ahead. It had been hard enough getting Nokummus into this barn. How could she travel any greater distance? But after a short trek into the brush to relieve herself, the old one was steadier on her feet and less winded. By late morning, she seemed to have regained some of her strength. Addie was heartened by this but reluctant to suggest the only solution to their difficulties that had occurred to her. Hard as she tried to think of something else, her thoughts kept going to her father's house outside the village, to the house she had lived in all of her life. If they crossed to the dunes, they'd be nearer to it than she'd been when she'd hidden in the abandoned shipyard. Still, even though it was a short trip across the river, it would be a long walk from wherever they could leave the canoe, too long for an old woman in a weakened condition. And Matilda. If they couldn't find the cat soon, they'd have to leave Matilda behind.

# twenty-eight

BEFORE THE SHORT SHADOWS in the pasture indicated noon, they had gathered their few intact possessions and begun the climb downhill to the waiting canoe. Addie carried most things, and Nokummus used a walking stick, planting it firmly every few steps when she needed to rest. Addie couldn't believe how long it took them to traverse a space she had routinely run up and down in what seemed like minutes. The burned parts of the *wetu* still smoldered and looked more like a heap of blackened refuse than a place where anyone had ever lived.

With Nokummus finally seated in the dugout, Addie ran back to look for Matilda. She called the cat in every way possible — a coaxing voice, with endearing nicknames — trying but not always succeeding in keeping the sense of urgency out of her voice. When she spotted Mr. Marshall's wagon, however, making its way to the island at low tide, she knew it was definitely time to leave. To avoid him, she had to push the canoe into deeper waters, which would make the crossing longer. But once launched, the craft began to swiftly penetrate the beds of whistling eelgrass, and all at once it seemed to Addie that the voyage possessed a preordained sense of purpose.

Nokummus didn't paddle, but Addie knew it was easier traveling with her in the boat than it would be when they reached the mainland. She tried not to think ahead to what might happen once they were on the road — an old Agawam trail that was still used as the most direct path to the fields and houses on the outskirts of town and to the town itself. She was worried about the exposure on such a path, on being discovered as the runaway daughter of Emerson Hayden.

When they landed on a spit of sand not far from the dunes through which she and Little Star used to ride, she dragged the canoe to a more sheltered spot. She was surprised to see clammers already at work farther down the beach. The tines of their forks caught the light; the sacks on their shoulders made them look hunchbacked and old. She gathered her heavy hair into both hands and hid it under the cap she'd worn the day she'd left her father's house. Dressed in the deerskin breeches made by Nokummus, she hoped again to be taken for a boy.

Nokummus seemed wistful and curiously uninvolved. She made no comments and offered no suggestions. When Addie spoke to her, the girl recognized the same kind of preaching monologue she had aimed at Jack when he was being petulant.

Still surrounded by marsh grass and uncertain where the path began, Addie settled Nokummus in a dry sandy place above the tide line and went in search of it. There was a wind, but it didn't cut to the bone like the ones of winter. Early, greener grasses could be seen sprouting from the sediment amid a brackish smell of salt and new growth; red-winged blackbirds perched in bare trees and swooped over her as if to display their scarlet markings. She passed through low dunes, under clusters of apple trees not yet in bloom, and across unending patches full of brambles that pulled at her clothing and scratched her face. There would be blueberries here in summer, and the notion caused her to smile and admit to a homesickness that she'd kept at bay all these months. She and Papa had been here before. She recognized the grove of white birch, the singular outcroppings of rock. Though she couldn't yet see the road itself, she knew exactly where it would be and how to get there. Buoyed by finding a familiar place and realizing how very close they were to the road, their first destination, she ran all the way back to where the Indian woman waited and pulled her to a standing position with both hands. Nokummus seemed puzzled and began to shake. Her fearful eyes searched Addie's face for the meaning of such exuberance.

"It's not far," Addie blurted out. "The path. It isn't far at all."

Forgetting for a moment that her grandmother was not well, Addie removed their belongings from the canoe and started off. When she didn't hear the shuffle of moccasins behind her, however, she turned, only to find that the old woman's feet were still planted in the sand where she'd left her.

"I cannot," Nokummus declared. "My body is too tired. The distance is too long."

"No," said Addie. "It isn't far at all to the path. You'll be all right. You'll see. We'll make it just fine."

"I cannot," Nokummus repeated in a voice that could barely be heard this time.

But *you* *have* *to*, thought Addie, even as she saw that the old woman's body was sinking of its own accord onto the strand where she'd been resting. She couldn't leave her here. There was no one she could ask for help. If only she still had Little Star. If only her father had never left or if he could magically return and save them both.

Addie returned to her grandmother, put down the things she was carrying, stooped low, and slowly settled the old woman onto her own back. When the girl stood up, it seemed at first as if she couldn't move. A sudden gasp escaped Nokummus's lips as she wound her frail arms around Addie's neck. With the girl's arms stretched backward to anchor her burden, they began to move as one through the outskirts of the marshes. Addie struggled to keep her footing through the dunes and needed to put down the old woman whenever there was a cleared and open space. At first Addie was surprised at how light Nokummus truly was. Not much harder to carry than a large bundle. But as the trip progressed, Addie's steps became slower, her back began to ache, and she wondered if this had, in fact, been the best solution. The distance to the path seemed so much longer when walking for two. Every little while Nokummus would ask, "How far?" And Addie would reassure her that it wouldn't be much farther. But it wasn't until she saw the top of a moving wagon through the trees that she knew they must be nearly there. She would have run to it if she could, but she did trudge more hopefully, even though it felt by now as if her chest and the arches of her feet were caving in.

When she saw at last an opening in the trees and the trail itself, not much wider than a footpath, she still had to find a place that was out of the way and safe where she could settle her grandmother and return for their belongings. A fallen log was the only thing that seemed possible at first, but across the road and a little ways into the brush, she found a large flat rock protected by trees that couldn't be seen by passersby.

Addie's trip back to the river was like a sprint in comparison to her labored trek with her grandmother on her back. But as she returned with their belongings, the haversack, baskets, and bulky parcels began to seem almost as heavy as Nokummus. How would she ever get everything, the two of them and their many bundles, all the way to the house in Essex?

She had hoped to arrive there before nightfall, but at dusk no plan had yet occurred to her, and Nokummus was stretched out and shivering on the surface of the rock, fast asleep. In desperation, Addie decided they'd need to travel the rest of the way in the same manner in which they'd covered the short distance to the road. The house, however, was at least five or six miles away, and Addie wasn't certain she was strong enough for such a task. She also didn't like leaving all their belongings here where someone was apt to discover them, and she dreaded coming all the way back again to collect them. Seeing no other solution, she was preparing to wake her grandmother and tell her the plan, when she heard the uneven clip-clop of a single horse that was poorly shod and the squeaky rustle of a cart being pulled on rusty wheels. She quickly stepped from behind the trees and out into the road, blocking the way. The cart driver squinted as if he couldn't believe his eyes and pulled up on the reins. The mangy horse neighed with irritation and came to an abrupt clattering stop.

"I've not a thing worth taking, son," the driver said as he held up one hand like a sign of truce. "Just bottles and rags. That's all, son. Just bottles and rags. They won't bring much."

"I'm not a robber, sir," Addie announced in a voice at least one register below her own. She was gratified the disguise was working and happy this was not someone she knew. "But I do want something from you."

"I told you. I haven't got a thing," said the man, "least-ways, not a thing worth taking."

"My grandmother and I," Addie continued. "We need to ride as far as the outskirts of town. She's feeling poorly."

The stranger looked over at the old woman, emerging from the trees with slow, faltering steps. He stroked his chin as if there had once been a beard there for just such rumina-tions. "I haven't laid eyes on a real live Injun in these parts for years and years, not since I was a boy. Just where you headed to?"

"To Bullock's field or thereabouts. It's a fair piece from here and much too far for her to walk."

"You'll have to get her up on board yerself. The rheuma-tism makes it hard to bend or lift."

Taking this remark to mean yes, Addie pushed the rags and bottles aside and lifted Nokummus into the cart. When she began to load their possessions on as well, the man shouted back at them.

"You didn't tell about the bric-a-brac. My poor old hoss can hardly pull this wagon, let alone a load like that and you two folks."

"It isn't far," said Addie. "And the two of us together, we're just skin and bones."

The last was nearly true. Their diet of the past few months had been sparse, with nothing that would serve to cushion them with fat.

By now the road ahead was being closed off by the dark, but then the man muttered something, peered into the night, and cracked his whip, and the horse began to trot along as if the path to town were written in his bones.

It was a bumpy, unsettling ride, and Addie had to grab for their possessions each time a wheel hit a hole. After too much of this, she pulled everything they owned to the back of the cart and forced the rags and bottles out of the way. They reeked of all manner of garbage and spirits, and clearly wouldn't be such a loss if they bounced into the woods.

Nokummus held her head in both hands as if it were loose and might fly off. The wide boards on the side of the cart did protect them from the wind, but a chill had descended as soon as the sun went down. In the blackness, Addie couldn't discern landmarks she might have recognized, so she stopped searching, pulled shawls around them both, and closed her eyes. Though the tremors of the cart made her feel a little sick, she soon became so lost in their strange and unpredictable pattern that when the rickety thing suddenly stopped, she was jolted from a half sleep.

"Here you be," called the man, reins dangling from one hand, "the edge of Bullock's field it is."

Still in a drowsy stupor, Addie stared into the shadowy landscape. Nothing seemed familiar except the lights from a cluster of houses in the distance. The homes were farther to the right than she remembered, but they looked to be the same ones that she'd always been able to see from her window. As on the night of her escape, there was little moonlight, but even this dim landscape didn't dampen her excitement at being so close to home again. She immediately stretched and yawned so as to feel less foggy and to get her bearings. Then she carefully lifted her grandmother and all their belongings to the ground. Grateful they'd found a way to travel this far, she quickly searched for the few dollars she'd hidden in her haversack so many months ago and gave one to the driver.

Nokummus shuffled over and handed the man a deerskin pouch. He chuckled to himself at both offerings. And as he cracked a whip and the horse and cart pulled away, he called over his shoulder, "In all my born days, I never seen a Injun so danged polite."

In the wake of silence that followed their departure, Nokummus draped herself against the farmer's fence, and Addie became concerned that her grandmother wouldn't be able to walk even the short distance that remained. But when she went to lift the old woman onto her back for a second time, Nokummus waved her away and said something short and angry in Wampanoag words that Addie couldn't understand. There was a renewed energy about her grandmother. When Addie touched her arm, she felt singed by what seemed to be a spark of the woman's former animation.

"I will walk this time," she said. "I know the way."

# twenty-nine

THEIR PROGRESS WAS SLOW. Having once decided she
could do this, however, Nokummus faltered only a few times
and had to come to a complete stop just once along the way.
Still, when the outline of the familiar roof came into view, it
seemed to Addie that it was a buoy, at the end of a lifeline.
She breathed a sigh of relief long before she'd set foot in
the yard. Even in the dark, her eyes went first to the place
where the coffin had been. In spite of the fact that John had
clearly told her the undertaker had come for it, she wanted
to find it there. The ground was already beginning to thaw,
and she couldn't help wondering when and where the burial
would be.

The hidden house key was still in the dirt of a broken
flowerpot, and as she dug it out and slipped it into the lock,

she was apprehensive that things wouldn't be the way that she'd left them. At first, it was hard to tell in the dark, but an immediate blast of stale air couldn't mask a damp repugnant odor. In a house that had been closed up so tightly for so long, Addie had expected something like this. She was grateful that none of the sickroom smells remained.

She rummaged in the small chiffonier until she found a candle and one of the friction matches that Papa kept. Many times she'd wished she'd had the foresight to carry a few of these on her travels. Now she was afraid to attract attention even from this flickering candlelight. When she was a young child, she'd wanted to live closer to town and other children. But Mama — Emmaline — had insisted that Papa build a house in this remote place away from neighbors of any kind. Addie had only recently come to understand a few of her reasons for this, one of which must have been to keep the eyes of the townspeople away. Now she felt safer knowing there was no one to notice their arrival. She definitely needed some light in order to see the state of the house and to find the source of the cloying odors.

"Mouse dirt," said Nokummus as she surveyed the floor and ran her hands along the dusty surface of things. "Mouse smell."

Of course. Even when the house had been fully occupied, a few field mice would often gain entry during the really cold months. This time they'd apparently invited all their relatives. Though there was movement in the shadows, she couldn't clearly see the little critters in this dimness or summon the energy to clean away what they'd left behind. Nokummus seemed too tired to care and tucked herself into the bed that had belonged to Emmaline, in no way resisting Addie's efforts to pile additional blankets on top of her. So exhausted that she was unconscious of her own hunger, Addie climbed to the loft and collapsed onto her trundle, pulling the familiar patchwork quilt up to her nose. She would search for firewood or try to light the new Glenwood coal stove in the morning. Several times she awoke in the night to sounds of scampering across the floor or to an awful creeping coldness that centered in her feet. By morning she couldn't wait to bring some comfort back into their lives.

She had to risk the fact that smoke rising from the chimney could be seen. When she learned how to load and start the coal stove, perhaps it would produce fewer fumes. But if she didn't do something right away to warm up the house, Addie was afraid that Nokummus's condition would get worse and that she herself might fall ill as well.

The curtains were as she had left them, pulled tightly across each window. But there was enough morning light seeping underneath them to illuminate the trails of mouse droppings, and there were a few bold mice still skittering along the baseboards and across the soapstone sink. She swatted at them with a broom and began to frantically sweep the mess they'd made right out the open door. Nokummus had risen to wipe tables and chairs, her expression as stoic as ever.

"Peppermint," said Addie all at once.

"What?"

"Peppermint oil. That's what Mama always used to scare away the field mice." She remembered how the house would sometimes smell of it for days. She began searching in cupboards and drawers but didn't find any until she went to check the food stores in the cellar. A number of Papa's carefully packaged soups had been broken into and nibbled. Some of the potatoes sported tiny teeth tracks. But the jars of preserved fruit and vegetables were intact as well as the bottled eggs. The dried fish was undisturbed in covered jars.

She found the tightly stoppered bottle of peppermint oil on a high shelf, and she took down a jar of peaches and a bag of walnuts for their breakfast. Last summer Papa had rented the peach tree from a nearby orchard for the whole season. They had spent many days picking the ripe fruit, with Jack playing with Matilda and running in circles at the base of the tree. Mama's fair hair had hung loose down her back. The hem of her light dress had been caught by the toe of her shoe as she tried to climb the ladder. Papa had caught her when she fell backward, and he'd waltzed her around as if she were a bride. It had been such a happy time. Such a sunny, faraway happy time.

When Addie came upstairs, Nokummus was standing by the loom and looking at it with amazement.

"That's Mama's loom," Addie said with a catch in her voice. "She used to weave all the time."

"That small white lady was not your mother," said Nokummus.

*But she was Mama*, thought Addie. She would always be Mama.

"She was the only mother I ever really knew," she told the old woman. "Surely you can understand that!"

"But she did not give life to you."

What her grandmother was saying was true. Addie had learned for herself that it was true. But she'd also been part of a family, and all its members were still very dear to her.

"I loved her," said Addie, and Nokummus bristled. She didn't tell her grandmother that she couldn't love White Moon, that she could not love someone whom she had never come to know. The dream of her own birth was becoming more and more faint, even though the connection she'd felt to the woman in it remained strong. Except for that connection, tales of her Wampanoag mother were just stories. This person Addie had become — sometimes she felt as if that girl were just a story, too.

# *thirty*

THE CLEAR SONG OF THE PHOEBE lifted Addie's spirits. Papa had called it the first bird of spring. Purple and white crocuses had begun to poke through in the garden beds, and there were unidentifiable green shoots here and there. When a pair of bobwhites arrived to provide their soft cooing sounds at dawn, Addie supposed it must be April. Nokummus affirmed this by identifying the Grass Moon. The old woman seemed further revived by her own observation. These past few weeks had, in fact, witnessed a return of some of her former vitality. Together, she and Addie had learned to operate the newfangled coal stove. Vented through the chimney, it did seem to produce less in the way of exhaust, and the coals turned to a bed of embers that spread an even heat.

Only the watchful eyes of John Tower had discerned that anyone was living here. He came by shortly after their return "to set and wind the clock," he said as he held out a loaf of fresh bread and a plucked chicken. She wondered if it was one of the ones she'd abandoned.

"I know about the burned wigwam," he said.

She felt a certain warmth travel through her at the thought that he was always watching over her, always seemingly aware of her comings and goings. That he never forgot. Addie almost couldn't contain her delight on seeing him again, but she didn't want to fuel Nokummus's silly ideas about his need for a wife.

"Yer lookin' a darn sight better," John told her at the door, "more like a girl should look."

She knew he meant it as a compliment, but she'd enjoyed wearing breeches and caps. Flustered, her hand went to her head, and she thought of what it might be like to wear her hair up like a lady or form it into curls over her ears like Miss Fitzgibbon and wondered if John would like the look of it if she did.

These past few days, she'd been dressing much as she used to — in a homespun dress over a chemise and quilted petticoat. Mama had even given fancy bell sleeves to the two dresses she'd stitched up last summer and put ribbon trim around the necks. Addie'd had to let out the "grow tucks" already, and she liked the way the skirts now flounced around her calves.

"You'll have to dress like the women of the town, too," she told Nokummus, "so they won't be suspicious of you if any of them come to call."

Her grandmother had grumbled at the notion but eventually spent some time taking apart a few old calico housedresses of Emmaline's and piecing and stitching them up again to fit her larger frame. Addie had helped her secure her massive mane of white hair into a prim bun at the nape of her neck, while her grandmother complained at the uncomfortable feel of it. But she refused to be encased in one of Emmaline's corsets, which didn't fit her solid shape anyway, or to be confined in a clean pair of the lady's drawers. Looking at her now, Addie could hardly recognize the native woman who'd traveled the countryside alone and lived in the woods.

But John obviously did. There was both surprise and disapproval in his eyes when he came into the front room and saw her bent over the stove. It was a curious look that made it clear he'd never expected to see her there. But then Addie remembered that he didn't know anything about the bark ceremony, the vision quest, or that this Indian woman was her grandmother.

"What should I tell folks if they begin to ask why she's here?" he said in a low voice.

"You can tell them I've returned with my grandmother. They'll think I did go to live with Emmaline's kin, the way you said."

"Not if they get a good look at her." John nodded in Nokummus's direction and spoke as if he thought that even if she did hear him, she couldn't understand his words. "They've seen this old woman around and about for years."

Nokummus picked up her head and stared him straight in the face.

"I am her true grandmother. And I speak English," she told him.

He bit his lip and cleared his throat but didn't apologize. His eyes pleaded with Addie for some explanation, but she didn't know where to begin. Would he understand if she told him that she'd always felt different and incomplete? She needed to make him believe that her journey, her insistence on living in the wild, and her attachment to Nokummus had been for purposes she now could openly recognize. But she couldn't explain it all to him here, in this room, in the place where Mama and Jack had died, and that Nokummus now occupied, body and spirit.

She took his arm and led him into the empty chicken yard. She thought of how much she missed Fleur and Little Star and the daily tasks of tending to them. Their absence continually pricked at her. As if in answer to her thoughts,

John said, "Just say when it is you want 'em, and I'll bring the animals back. Oh, not the chickens. Most of them been et already."

Before she could begin the explanation she'd been crafting in her head, John took a letter from his pocket. "Mrs. Woodberry gave my ma this post," he said, "knowing how yer pa was on the *Metropolis* and all, and how you and me was friends. Ma says there's people still suspect I have a way to find you." He held up the letter. "I thought you'd want to hear what's in it."

The letter was from Stephen Woodberry to another shipwright and was dated January 23, 1850. Addie thought that it must have come overland to get here so quickly. Aware that she was the better reader, she took it from John's hands to read aloud.

"We arrived at San Francisco the 16th and at Sacramento last night. We had 120 days' passage from St. Catherine's. Off Cape Horn we had our topsails reefed for twenty days. We sprang our jibboom and fore topmast. Sent down four top gallant mast and made the rest of the voyage without it. We passed our time making dirks, daggers, slung shots, and pistol cases and now find they are of little use. Thomas Foster of Salem, 2nd mate of ship Ocean, condemned at St. Catherine's, worked his passage out with us. The ships provisions were not as we expected.

Considerable of the bread spoiled. I do not advise you to come here for I think it would cost $400 or $500 for passage from Beverly. The Company have consigned the vessel to Peirce, Willis, and Fay, vessel and cargo. Vessel to bring $6,000. The Company has broken up. We sold one old and five little pigs for $100, I think they would have brought $15 in Beverly. We start for the mines in a few days."

If the Metropolis had been sold as that man claimed, how would Pa get home? Even if he were successful in the mines, he'd have to find another way back.

"Story is there's hundreds of vessels been abandoned in San Francisco harbor. Men just up and left 'em there to go into the mines. They say the bay is filled with bare masts."

This news and the letter's contents hit Addie like a physical blow. She all but doubled over in shock at what she was hearing. Yet the fact there hadn't been a recent letter from her father had made her suspicious that he had no good news to report. If she wrote to him now, where would she send it and what would she say? Was any of it possible, all the things that Nokummus had warned her about? Could he be hurt or sick somewhere? Could he even be dead? This complete and utter disconnection from him hurt worse than a bad tooth.

"Addie?" said John. "You look all swimmy-headed."

She put both hands to her cheeks. Her head had begun to pound. All the things she'd wanted to tell John, the explanation for everything, had drained from her mind.

"This thing you said about that old Indian being your grandmother," John remarked at last. "When'd you come up with that notion?"

She held her breath and tried to clear her thoughts. When she answered him, her voice was steady, but her reason wavered as she tried to organize her words into something coherent. "It's no notion. It's the absolute truth."

"Prove it," he said.

She knew he wasn't going to accept as proof the memories from her fevered dream. They'd played together as babies. At her house, Mama had been the one to pass out sugar buns and to watch over their games. He was bound to feel certain of who her mother was. Convincing him otherwise didn't even seem to be a possibility. But having him believe her meant everything. If he refused to, then no one else would believe her either.

There was a time coming, and she suspected it wasn't far off, when someone other than John would find that she and Nokummus were living here. As if to tempt their fate, she'd become less cautious about appearing in the yard in daylight. She'd even hung some clothes to dry on the line outside, and Nokummus had traveled more than once into the woods to dig for roots. She knew that if they were going to live here undisturbed, she had to find the proof that John demanded and she needed to find it soon.

John had brought them other news, news that had been the reason he'd come looking for her back in Essex. Clive had been bragging about how he'd burned down what he called the old Injun's tepee. He continued to claim to know that Addie had been living there, too, but no one believed him.

"Clive's skiff got swamped when he took off from the island," said John. "He had to wade in icy water to the shore, and he's spooked now that the Injun cast some kind of spell."

Addie laughed. It was the perfect comeuppance. Telling John was one thing, but he wouldn't be bragging to others about the fire anytime soon.

"I was sure it was Clive," she told John before he left. "And I know he did it because of who I am."

"Just who are you?" he said, clearly miffed. "Just who in tarnation do you think you are?"

"I'm half Wampanoag," she declared in a voice that surprised her for the pride in it. "It's what I've been trying to tell you. It's what I've had to discover about myself."

His look was dark and angry. "So you're claiming to be some half-breed squaw. Is that it? And that your mamaw's that old Indian in there?" He pointed to the house, then stood without talking for a while as if, having presented this challenge, he was waiting for her to respond. When she didn't, he spit in the dirt, turned, and walked away without looking back. A slap across the face could not have hurt as much.

His words and that awful look of contempt stayed with her. It hadn't occurred to her that if she finally found out the truth about herself, others close to her wouldn't accept it, or if they did, they'd be like Clive and think the less of her. Until Pa came home and could straighten things out, there was nothing and no one to back up what she claimed. What was worse was this terrible feeling that she'd seriously disappointed the person she'd most wanted on her side. She couldn't bear to think that things would never be the same again between them.

# thirty-one

AT SUPPER, Nokummus merely picked at the chicken. She pushed aside the boiled potatoes. At first Addie thought that John's visit must have unsettled her. But when she rose to clear the plates away and brushed by her, the heat that emanated from the old woman's body was startling. And when she pressed her palm against the grooves of her grandmother's forehead, it was like touching a saddle that had been left in the sun.

"Come along," Addie said as she guided her back to bed and loosened her clothing. She hadn't noticed a cough. Her grandmother hadn't complained of any aches or pains. She had actually been unusually quiet all day.

Nokummus lifted one hand to her neck and stroked it. "My throat is like fire," she rasped.

Addie panicked. Throat distemper. That was how the deadly flux had begun. With an inflammatory fever and sore throat. She hadn't known what to do then, and she still didn't know what steps to take. But she'd later heard how some of the survivors had gone for the doctor at the first signs. And she remembered how Mama kept telling her it wasn't necessary, and how before she knew it, it had been too late.

An unexpected snow had been falling steadily since noon, and there was an unusual accumulation for a spring storm. They had eaten an early supper, so there were still a few hours of daylight left. Certain that this little snow squall would not amount to anything and desperately worried about her grandmother's worsening condition, Addie made sure Nokummus was comfortable and warm. She unearthed her own heavy woolen cloak and the boots she'd already put away for the season, and started for Dr. Perkins's house. She recalled it as a tiny yellow house at the edge of a gully, three or four miles away. Its funny squat turret was always lit, and she was sure she'd recognize it even in the dark.

She headed in the direction of the gully, pulling tight her woolen bonnet and holding the collar of her cloak against her face to resist the biting wind and pelting snow. The first mile or so was not too difficult, but she wasn't at all happy about this return of winter. How much easier this trek would have been only yesterday. Yet yesterday she hadn't harbored this crushing fear that someone else close to her was about to die. To distract herself, she thought of birds safe in their trees or squirrels huddled in their holes, but she couldn't see much of anything but large stretches of white, edged in the dark specters of evergreens.

When she believed she had come to a ridge that she remembered as being a few miles south of the gully, the snow began coming at her in blinding sheets that obscured everything even a few feet in front of her and made her gasp for breath. She held up a mittened hand but couldn't discern its outline. Turning to see how far she'd come, she couldn't even pick out the light she'd made certain to leave in the window. The dark had not yet fallen, but this blizzard of white made every landmark invisible and closed her into a frightening world whose boundaries were the edge of her extremities. There was no point in standing still, and she couldn't clearly see anything behind her or sense how far she'd come, so she mushed ahead, feeling like a blind animal attuned to any natural sound or sense — the flutter of a wing, an imperceptible rise or fall in the landscape.

Papa had always said she had an uncanny sense of direction, and she stopped to say a silent prayer that this was true. There was nothing from which she could get her bearings. She regretted leaving Nokummus sick and alone. She imagined her calling out in the night and getting no response.

Addie even envisioned some passerby finding her own frozen and lifeless body when the storm was over. But she kept trudging ahead for what seemed like an endless space of time until she ran into a rim of trees. Thinking that if she kept to the edge of them, they'd eventually lead her to the gully, she waved her arms around like a madwoman and reached out to keep contact with the branches of the small firs all along the way. The fierce gale pushed against her with such force, and her steps were so labored, that after she'd managed to go even a little way, she felt bruised all over.

After so much of this struggle that she thought she must have veered off somewhere, a tiny pinprick of light appeared below her, as if radiating from a trench, and she fixed her eyes upon it until it began to grow in size and brightness. She moved steadily toward it, and, suddenly aware that the ground was beginning to slope, stumbled into what she realized all too late was the gully she'd been looking for and that she was suddenly flying over the rim of it. The snow cushioned her fall, and her roll down the little hill was soft. After the shock of her tumble, she looked up to see that she'd landed in someone's backyard, and she hoped it belonged to the doctor. What he might think of this chattering apparition in white didn't enter her mind. She simply picked herself up and slogged to the back door.

"There's a sick old woman in my house," she said when

the doctor's wife peered out. "I need Dr. Perkins to come with me."

"My land," said the lady. "You're a walking snowman. You'll have chilblains or worse if we don't get you out of those clothes."

Addie was given hot broth and wrapped in blankets before the fire, while the doctor seemed to be trying to make sense of who she was and where she wanted him to go. Her tongue was so frozen she could hardly form the words she needed, and she kept blubbering like a little child, great tears splashing into the mug of soup.

"So you're Emerson's girl," he said at last. "I'm right sorry about the passing of your kin."

"I should have come to fetch you," Addie blurted out between sobs. "I should have known how sick they were."

He patted her shoulder. "No telling if it would have done a bit of good, child. Sometimes my medicine works; sometimes it doesn't. I'm not a magician."

Then he smiled in a knowing and satisfied way that Addie found confusing. "Get her some of Sally Ann's clothes, Elizabeth," he said to his wife. "We'll take the cutter."

The storm had subsided by the time they started out, but Addie was still cold to the bone. Snow flew off the horse's hooves like sparkling dust, and there was a hush to the landscape that made her feel safe. There was even a large top on the doctor's sleigh to protect them. When she thought of Nokummus, however, she became so impatient with the slow trot and the doctor's easy manner that she wanted to scream. At one point they left the road and started through the fields, and Addie was relieved to see the candle she'd put in the window. She willed them to go faster, but the doctor kept the horse at an easy pace, turning minutes into what seemed to Addie like the slow stretch of hours. When at length she jumped down from the buggy and burst through the door, she ran to Nokummus like a small child who'd been torn from her mother. The old woman appeared to have been asleep all the while, unaware of the storm or of Addie's absence, and she looked at the doctor with cloudy eyes full of suspicion at first and then clearly with recognition.

"Mary Goodrich," he said on seeing who his patient was, "what's this I hear about you feeling poorly?"

Addie was surprised that he knew her grandmother and amazed that she was acquainted with him as well. But then she remembered how the old woman had peddled her vegetables and clams all over the town and was probably not a stranger to anyone hereabouts. And for some reason, he didn't seem to think it odd that she was living here in Addie's house. He looked at her throat, felt her forehead, and gave her a tonic to gargle with.

"I know," he said when she started to resist. "You probably

have a potion of your own devising for just such ailments. But I've tried your remedies in the past, so just this once give mine a try."

"Keep her warm," he said to Addie. "Give her plenty of things to drink. She'll be fit as a fiddle in no time."

"I was worried about the flux," Addie told him as she walked him to the door. "Are you sure she doesn't have the flux like Mama had?"

"It's nothing near as serious as that. You do exactly what I said, and your grandmother will be just fine."

At first Addie wasn't sure if she'd heard the words right. How could this man whom she'd only met once or twice in her life be aware of her secret? Was there more of a resemblance between Nokummus and herself than she was aware of?

"Didn't think I knew that, did you?" he said. "And I knew your birth mother, too. But not for long. Your father called me much too late to save her."

The hands she'd felt upon her head in the dream, the ones that had lifted her into the light. They had belonged to this quiet, unassuming man who knew more about her than anyone in the world besides Nokummus and her father. She'd needed proof and here it was, proof that had apparently existed all her life in that funny yellow house just over the gully.

# thirty-two

JUST AS DR. PERKINS HAD SAID, in two or three days Nokummus was eating again and restless to be out-of-doors. There'd been a short span of warmer weather that had diminished the snow cover and laid bare wide stretches of dead grass. Trees were budding but not yet in full leaf. When the old woman decided to leave the house and walk into the woods to search for fiddlehead ferns, Addie saw it as a good sign. She was less cautious about prying eyes now that she knew someone of importance who could vouch for the relationship between the two. A girl could live with her grandmother, after all. It was the most natural thing in the world.

Nokummus seemed renewed when she returned with a basketful of fiddleheads. They were the color of jade, springy to the touch, and tightly curled. She'd also found a patch of morel mushrooms, and she lightly fried the two together for their supper and sprinkled the dish with sea salt. The act of cooking and the fresh taste of the food seemed to cheer her even further. But as twilight fell, Addie found her grandmother huddled by the window and staring out into the dim landscape. Usually her hands were busy with some task, and she'd be taking advantage of the last of the failing natural light for any close work. She didn't turn when Addie stood near her, not even when she came close enough to lay a hand on her shoulder. Addie resisted the urge to put an arm around her, for she knew by now that her grandmother didn't like to be touched and had allowed it, more for Addie's sake than her own it seemed, only when she'd been feeling completely bereft.

"Are you all right?" Addie asked her. "You haven't suffered a chill?"

"No. No chill," said Nokummus.

"You seem . . ." Addie began. She wasn't quite sure how to describe the woman's mood. "You seem troubled."

"I have a big worry."

"How big?"

"Too big."

"Too big to share it?"

Nokummus grunted a sound so indistinct it could have meant either yes or no.

"Are you going to tell me what it is?"

Nokummus didn't answer her. Instead she began to complain bitterly. "The rooms here are too large. This house is too cold."

Addie thought that her grandmother's complaints were peculiar. It was a little house; the weather was much warmer now; there wasn't the constant wind that had buffeted the island. And she hadn't grumbled once during that entire frigid winter they'd just spent together.

"Summer will be here soon," she said. *Papa will be coming home*, she thought.

"In summer we will go to the ancestral home," Nokummus announced. Her look was set but expectant. She searched Addie's face.

Since the bark ceremony, Nokummus had alluded to this idea several times. So the fact that she would assume Addie would be going with her to Chappiquiddic was not a complete surprise. Addie had tried time and again to show a lack of enthusiasm for the idea.

"It's too far from here, and"—this time she said her unspoken thoughts aloud—"Papa will be coming back. I need to be here for Papa." She was still angry at him—for keeping her true identity from her, for treating Nokummus like a stranger—but to her he had always been the kindest, the most caring person in the world, and she needed to hear his side of things, even if it seemed impossible that she could ever be satisfied with his answers.

"You will welcome back the man who left you alone?"

Of course she would welcome him back. How she longed to see him, to be held against his heart.

"He didn't think I was alone. He had no reason to think that. All the food we've been eating—he made certain it was put by for Mama and me and Jack for the winter."

"But however much you desire his return, such a long journey as your father's contains many trials and dangers. If he does not come back, you will need me more than you do now. You will need the tribe."

"No," said Addie. She refused to even consider such a possibility. Papa would be coming back. They could all live together here in Essex.

"And you are a special child. You are Wampanoag."

Addie had come to know and believe the last part.

"And like your grandfather, you can be a leader. The tribe needs you."

"Tell me about my grandfather." It seemed odd to Addie that Nokummus had never mentioned him.

"He died of a bad sickness when still a young man," said Nokummus. "Like White Moon, he died before he could fulfill his destiny. His days as a spiritual leader were short. But you. You are a healthy young woman. Your days as *pauwau* can be long and full of wisdom."

"Oh, no. I can't be what you want. I don't even know the language that you — that the tribe speaks."

"You are a smart girl. You can learn. And many of us speak English."

Addie was also certain that she could learn the language. But Nokummus wanted her to learn a whole new life, a whole new place. To leave her father.

As when she'd tried so hard to argue her way out of the bark ceremony, she strained every facet of her brain to think of reasons to give her grandmother as to why the old woman's plan was not a good idea. Yes, Addie'd like to see the ancestral lands someday. She'd like to meet her uncles and cousins. But she didn't want to leave behind the things she knew and loved.

"Hobbamock," she said at last. "I never met with Hobbamock. He never made a pact with me the way you said he would."

Nokummus was standing stock-still, but Addie could see from the way she'd quickly drawn into herself that she was thinking hard about what Addie had just said. Perhaps, thought the girl, this was the big worry her grandmother had complained about.

To Addie, the fact that the Warrior Spirit had not acknowledged her had to be validation that she was not ordained to be a tribal leader in the way Nokummus had planned. Her grandmother's sudden dark silence convinced the girl that the old woman was being assailed by these same thoughts.

"It must be a big mistake," said Nokummus. "We must go to the tribal elders and find the reason for this big mistake."

"What if," asked Addie, "it was no mistake at all?"

"That is not possible," said Nokummus. She rose from her chair by the window and brushed at her apron as if to sweep away a lapful of invisible things. She lit a candle and placed it in the window well. Its flame sent spines of light across her face. They pulled at the craggy hollows and brightened the haze over her eyes, making her appear as wise and mysterious as she'd first seemed to Addie. The girl was suddenly frightened at the prospect that this strong Indian woman she had come to know as her grandmother might in fact possess some mystic Wampanoag power to work her will and effect the changes in her granddaughter's life that the woman so fervently desired.

She sat silently in a chair across the room and looked down at the wide floorboards as if they held an answer. Nokummus was quiet, too. The only sound was the loud tick of the clock and the chime as it struck the hour. They sat this way long enough for Addie's snarled mind to begin to unravel the knots that had held her unexpressed thoughts and feelings for some time. If she acknowledged these thoughts, she knew they would be convincing evidence that she didn't really fit anywhere. Her father had often said she had the dimples of his English mother and the zest for life of his Scottish grandmother. With complete clarity at last, she recognized exactly what this meant: her Wampanoag blood was not pure. She was a half-breed in each of the worlds she straddled. She was convinced that was the reason Hobbamock had not appeared to her. There was no pact he could possibly make with a half-breed that would elevate her to be a leader of the tribe. What could she say that would explain this to Nokummus? Why hadn't she figured it out herself?

"There is no rule," said Nokummus when confronted with this abhorrent notion.

"Hobbamock makes the rules," said Addie. "And he didn't pick me."

"Perhaps he will change his mind."

"How will we know if he does?" asked Addie, annoyed at her grandmother's refusal to let go of this idea. But the woman grew more and more testy.

"I don't know," Nokummus blurted out finally. "I cannot know everything. We will have to wait and see."

# thirty-three

ADDIE LISTENED to the splash and patter of rain on the roof and didn't open her eyes. It thrummed a comforting rhythm that almost put her back to sleep. But when she suddenly remembered that John might bring Little Star and Fleur today, she threw the bedclothes from her with such force they slipped to the floor. She wondered if he would still come, given the way in which he'd left last time. The boards were noticeably warmer on her bare feet than they'd been even yesterday. She stretched to peer out the high window in the loft, eyes peeled for any sight of the trio. But there was nothing moving even in the pastures beyond.

Nokummus was already up, stirring cornmeal mush on the coal stove. She poured a bowl for Addie and laced it with the honey Papa had collected the previous June. It was too early for fresh berries, so she sprinkled the mixture with dried cranberries that Emerson Hayden had put by as well. The old woman had scorned the man's carefully stored provisions for some time but eventually began to help herself to them regularly without any apparent thought to who'd been the provider.

All morning, Addie stayed by the window and waited on John's promise. Shortly before noon, she began to think he'd either been called to do a shift in the yards or was staying away on purpose as she'd feared. She climbed to the loft again to look out the high window, but there wasn't anyone on foot or even a wagon in sight. With the animals away, she hadn't felt truly at home. She needed them to come back so she could finally come to terms with all the other missing pieces of her life here.

"A watched pot will not boil," said Nokummus when Addie continued to fidget and pace. Addie remembered Mama saying that, too, each time the girl was impatient for something to happen. It was jarring to have the same expression come from the mouth of her Indian grandmother. She wondered where Nokummus had heard it, and it made her feel that maybe there could have been a kind of kinship between the two women if Mama had lived.

•  •  •

When it became later and later in the day, and John and the animals had failed to appear, Addie stopped looking for them. She took up her embroidery and pricked away at the roses and tendrils of the pattern. Emmaline had taught her this skill last summer. The birds and flowers that Mama had traced on the cloth were delicate and fanciful, the threads all shades of pinks and greens. It was such a true expression of her stepmother, and Addie was determined to finish it.

She had just begun to stitch the darker green of a leaf when she heard a scratching noise at the door and ran to open it wide. Expecting to see John and the animals, she looked out to the yard. But then a loud meow made her glance down at her feet, where Matilda was hunched, strangely aloof and skittish. When Addie gave an excited cry and bent to pick her up, the cat ran off into the bushes.

"Here, kitty, kitty," Addie called in the softest, sweetest voice she could muster.

Nokummus came up behind her and put a dish of chicken scraps on the stoop.

"Why is she afraid of me?" asked Addie. She was thrilled and amazed to have Matilda back again but devastated that the cat had run from her like that.

"Your cat has been living in the wild," said Nokummus. "She has much fear."

"Fear of me?" Addie was offended but also astonished that the cat had survived so long on Hog Island by herself and that she had been able to make her way back to them. She couldn't believe that Matilda was now afraid of her. "All I want to do is take care of her and keep her safe."

"She was left alone," said Nokummus. "She does not know the reason why."

"But we had to leave," said Addie. "We didn't have a choice."

"And in a few days, perhaps, she will forgive you. You must wait."

Addie knew what it felt like to be abandoned, even when you knew the reason. She had sympathized with her father's need to leave, but now she wondered if she could ever be as forgiving of him as she hoped Matilda would be of her. She was worried that John would arrive with the horse and cow and further scare away the cat.

"We will leave the door open like this," said Nokummus as she braced it with a stick to provide a smaller opening, "and bring the food inside." She put the chicken scraps well into the room.

It was an hour or so before the cat did venture after the food, and then she took small portions with her teeth and carried them to a corner, one paw holding the scraps, one raised to protect them. If either Addie or Nokummus stirred, Matilda ran to another corner. It made Addie sad to see her good-natured cat so defensive and fearful. When the animal had her belly full at last, however, she fell fast asleep in a pool of afternoon sun.

John didn't arrive with Fleur and Little Star until twilight. As Addie ran to throw her arms around the necks of both animals, Little Star whinnied, and she felt reassured that they knew her and would be happy to be back in the familiar stalls that she'd filled with clean hay. She had the sudden urge to throw her arms around John's neck as well and hold him tight, but she feared his reaction.

"Sorry it took so long," he said. "I had to walk into town to the Jacob Story yard and then high-tail it all the way back home to get these two." She was relieved to see that his voice was kindly as ever when he spoke.

Already she was planning how she'd milk Fleur early the next morning and ride out to the dunes with Little Star. It would be good to have fresh milk again. Distracted by her thoughts, she barely listened to what John was saying until he repeated part of what he'd been trying to tell her. "The day after tomorrow," he said. "They're going to bury your mother and Jack the day after tomorrow."

Her mind went suddenly black, as if the two had just died

all over again. Burial was such a final act. Burial was necessary she knew, but so very final. She felt as if she couldn't breathe.

"It'll be early morning," he continued. "You gonna be there? I can come get you. My ma is coming, too."

Of course she would be there. But this was something she needed to do all by herself with no one to help or support her. When she told Nokummus, it was clear that she understood, but she didn't know what the townsfolk would think. She didn't care any longer, however. Dr. Perkins was living proof of who she was and who her grandmother was, too. But she didn't want to be questioned or fawned over or to be the object of sympathy.

Addie decided it would soon be time to give John the proof he'd asked for, to tell him what the doctor had revealed to her, and she would fend off any busybodies at the cemetery with the truth of things.

The fact that Little Star was carrying her into town on a grim errand instead of along the beach dimmed but didn't extinguish her joy at being astride her once again. She'd missed the smell of her sweat, her rough mane against her face when she bent down to urge her along, the way her own hair flew behind her like one dark wing when she galloped.

Close to town, she brought her down to a trot. She took the road to the left just before the cemetery and tied the horse to a tree near the ridge at the back of the burial grounds that overlooked the river. Before she had turned, she could see a few buggies pulled up to the side of the main road. She wasn't surprised that there weren't more people. Mama had had few friends, and most everyone who did come would probably be there because of her father. Seeing an opportunity to stay out of the way entirely and not be noticed, she kept to the trees and watched the proceedings from this distance. The grave itself had been dug close to the school, and this pleased her. Jack would hear the children just as she'd imagined. But when the coffin was actually put into the ground, a silent cry filled her throat and she curled over in grief. She held her ears against the awful splatter of dirt being thrown against wood.

The service was short; the minister was someone she had never seen before. Only the trail ends of his sentences reached her, things like *peace* and *everlasting* and *reward*. She failed to see how such an early death could be a reward for anything. When the small group dispersed back to their traps and buggies, she went to mount Little Star again but a hand held her back.

"Miss Fitzgibbon!" exclaimed Addie.

"I noticed you over in the trees. For sure and all, I wasn't certain you'd come."

Her lilting brogue brought back the many happy days in the schoolroom. Addie wanted to run to her, but she kept the reins in her hand and stayed back.

"Where have you been, girl?"

There was so much to tell, so much that her teacher might not understand. For a little while, Addie felt as if their roles had been reversed.

At first she hesitated to tell it all, but then it was as if an ebb tide was carrying words from her throat and spilling them into the air. By the time she was finished, Miss Fitzgibbon had heard about the journey in the night, her time in the shipyard, and the days on Hog Island. And about Nokummus. She'd told her all about Nokummus and the bark ceremony and what Addie had discovered about herself. Addie was breathless and spent at the end of it all. And when Miss Fitzgibbon looked at her with eyes full of concern and care, Addie was moved to reveal what she hadn't voiced to another soul. "So I'm a half-breed wherever I go. I don't fit in anywhere."

The young woman reached out and pulled her close.

"Oh, my dear, you're bound to learn," she said, "there's them that judge you by the sound of your voice as much as by the color of your skin, don't you know. For instance, have you noticed many Irish in these parts?"

Addie had never thought about it. She'd always loved the sound of her teacher's voice.

"Sure and it was hard to even find a room to let. And people thought I was puttin' on airs when I claimed to be a teacher instead of a hired girl."

"I didn't know."

"Come back to school, Addie. You're a wise young girl with a good mind. You shouldn't be spending all your time on needlework and farming and the like."

She wanted to tell Miss Fitzgibbon that each day on the island had been an adventure full of things she'd had to learn just to survive. But what she really hungered for now were the things that could be found only in books. And she needed to give Nokummus a reason that she would understand for why Addie couldn't return to Chappiquiddic with her. The girl continued to worry over how she could follow her heart and still not alienate this old woman who had taught her so much and had provided the answers she'd desperately needed to find.

Miss Fitzgibbon brushed the hair back from Addie's face before helping her mount Little Star. She watched horse and rider trot down the slope to the path.

"Just be who you are," she called after the girl. "Be all that you are."

# thirty-four

ADDIE RODE LITTLE STAR as fast as she could all the way
back home, barely stopping to water her when they reached
her stall. She pushed open the door to the house and climbed
to the loft, passing right by Nokummus without a word. The
old woman gave her a glance but then went back to her work.
She'd been making baskets again since finding the right grasses
nearby. Her fingers didn't hesitate at her task.

At dusk, Addie came downstairs. Her hair was tangled, her
eyes lusterless and red-rimmed. She had fallen asleep with her
face on her hands, and there were streaks from the imprint
of her fingers along one cheek. When she tried to eat the vegetable stew that Nokummus put before her, she found she
couldn't swallow.

As the light slowly seeped from the room, Addie continued to sit by the plate of food that had grown cold. No one got up to light a candle. Nokummus's voice in the darkness seemed to come from far away.

"Grief is for the living," she said. "Souls who pass to the spirit world are not troubled. Fields are always green. Harvests are plentiful. Hunting is good."

To Addie, what her grandmother depicted sounded a lot like the heaven that people spoke about in church. She hoped there was such a place. It seemed to her that hope was what she had lived on since those terrible days in the autumn — hope that Mama and Jack would live, hope that she could survive on her own until Papa came back, hope that she might finally discover what it was that made her feel so restless and different. Hope had been crushed in the first instance, and she wondered now why it hadn't killed her spirit. Perhaps it was because some of the time it had seemed as if she was on an amazing journey and would return to things just as they were. And even though she'd ultimately discovered that this was only a childish dream, it had helped to hold her grief at bay. Faced with the conclusive event that she'd witnessed this morning, and finally aware of the significance of all that had happened and of her uncertain future, she'd been consumed by despair.

She could hear Nokummus rustling through the rooms as she prepared for the night. The swish of water in the basin, the creak of the bed as she lowered her body into it, the soft sound of quilts being plumped were all that Addie allowed into her mind as she rested her head upon the cold table. After a while, she had no more tears, and there were no longer any sounds, just a blank and dreamless sleep.

She could tell that the morning was bright even before she opened her eyes. When she did, she looked up from a puddle of warm sun. Her face was stiff from crying, her back sore from being bent over all night. She stood and stretched and felt body parts moving back into place and growing flexible again. Still burdened by the events of yesterday, she couldn't help being grateful for this new day. It was what Pa had taught her to do, and it had become a habit. No amount of sorrow or plain old feeling sorry for herself was likely to change that.

She washed her face and brushed her hair, tying it back as if she was about to clean the house. Not finding Nokummus in any of the rooms, she opened the door to look out across the fields toward the woods. It wasn't uncommon for the old woman to go in search of wild things very early in the morning. But what greeted Addie were John's mother, Mrs. Tower, and two ladies from the town in day dresses and bonnets — Mrs. Bright and the younger of the two, Miss Abigail Wonson. Addie'd seen them both a few times at her family's infrequent attendance at church and socials. Mrs. Bright was Fanny's mother, and she presently had a simpering look that didn't translate into either a grimace or a smile but something in between; Miss Wonson kept her lips pressed firmly into a straight line and held her gloved hands at her waist. Mrs. Tower had her two youngest in tow. They were already chasing a flock of crows and playing tag.

"May we come in, dear?" asked Mrs. Bright without so much as a greeting of any kind.

"Of course," said Addie, as she tried hard to think of the proper thing to do when someone came to call. Mama had rarely had visitors, and she would become all twittery and unnerved when she did. Surely that wasn't the demeanor Addie wanted to adopt. If she knew how to brew coffee, she would have offered that, but she didn't want to make the poor women sick. Instead she simply offered them chairs, and she herself sat on a footstool.

"I told you everything was just fine here," said Mrs. Tower, an eye fixed on the window and what she could see of the yard and her children.

"But why weren't you at the service, child?" Mrs. Bright began. "Such a sad occasion. So hard to think that your papa probably still doesn't know."

"What could he do if he did?" said Addie, and Mrs. Bright exchanged a look of shock with Miss Wonson.

"But to have no family members in attendance. I said to Prudence — Mrs. Tower — I said, 'That just isn't right.' And she told me how you were living here again, and I said, 'That can't be,' and she said, 'Oh, yes, most assuredly,' and that your grandmother was with you, and I said, 'Well, that's something I'll have to see for myself.'"

"I was at the service, Mrs. Bright," Addie said. She hesitated, not knowing how to go on. "I didn't want to stand . . . too close. I didn't know what to say to people. And, yes, my grandmother is living with me now." She crossed her fingers that Nokummus would stay away until these two busybodies had left. The story she'd hoped John had conveyed to anyone who asked was that this was a grandmother on her mother's side.

"Where is the lady?" asked Miss Wonson.

"She's in the woods, I believe, gathering . . . mushrooms," said Addie. "It's an interest of hers."

"Mushrooms," mused Mrs. Bright. "I myself do love a good morel. They say there's a patch surprising large by Traver's pond."

"That's probably where she is right now. I wouldn't wait. She sometimes spends all day at it."

The two women exchanged looks again that were easy to decipher and that showed they weren't at all sure they should believe this strange, precocious child.

"And why aren't you in school?" asked Abigail. It appeared to Addie as if this younger woman had been designated to ask all the important questions.

"I will be going back very soon," the girl said, even though she hadn't yet had any discussion with Nokummus about returning.

"Addie's always been a fine student," said Mrs. Tower.

The women glanced at the open copy of Sir Walter Scott on the table and the illuminated book of poems that had been Mama's, and they seemed reassured.

"You must understand," said Mrs. Bright. "We certainly don't mean to pry, but it is passing strange that you'd disappear all that while like you did and turn up with a relative no one has even heard of."

"Passing strange, indeed," echoed the inquisitor.

"I suppose it must be," answered Addie. She knew her situation was certainly not usual, and that if anyone actually knew the truth of things, it would be even more difficult for them to understand. Sometimes she didn't understand it herself. What she truly feared was that even if she could convince Nokummus to stay here with her, these busybodies would do something to prevent it.

"I do wish the lady would return soon," said Mrs. Bright. "Fanny is playing a little recital on the violin shortly. She'll have a fit if I come in late."

Mrs. Tower looked over at Addie.

"How are you, dear?" she asked. "You're looking so grown-up."

Addie smiled at this. She certainly felt changed in many ways but hadn't known that it showed.

"And I need to fetch a skein or two of yarn from Edna Babson," chirped Miss Wonson. "She's expecting me."

After many awkward moments of silence during which Nokummus did not make an appearance, Mrs. Bright said, "Oh, my. There'll be a buggy by the road for me in less than half an hour." She twisted her handkerchief and blew her nose. "Mr. Bright will not want to wait. You can be most assured of that."

The two impatient ladies continued to fidget and watch the clock, and Mrs. Tower left the room from time to time to check on a crying or rambunctious child.

Meanwhile, Matilda had taken her morning meal to the corner to protect it savagely, eyes gleaming like an animal's in the night. Both of the women in a hurry were obviously shaken when they noticed her there. Mrs. Tower rose with them as they got up and moved warily toward the door, while Addie stifled her relief and turned the knob for them. This time what met her view was Nokummus trudging back from the woods. She was moving slowly and still quite a distance from the house. In one of Emmaline's altered dresses and with her hair pinned back, she looked for all the world like any old woman from these parts.

"Oh, dear," said Mrs. Bright. "It's bound to be some time before she makes it across that field. We really shouldn't wait."

"I'll stay and pay your respects," said Mrs. Tower as she gripped an arm of each squirming child.

"Oh, would you, Prudence?" asked Mrs. Bright, seemingly consoled that her trip here had not been in vain.

It wasn't until the two started off in the opposite direction, the distance between them and Nokummus growing with each step, that Addie's stomach released the knots that had been forming.

"You had the whole town scared most to death last winter," said Mrs. Tower when the ladies were out of earshot. She released one child and gathered the smallest into her arms. "But then John told me you were with Mrs. Goodrich, and I knew you'd be just fine."

"You know her? I mean really know her?"

"Have known her all the years since you were born. A wise lady. She's been devoted to you since the very start."

"And my real mother. Did you know her, too?"

"I did. But she was here such a short time. Most folks don't remember."

When Nokummus finally approached, it was clear the two women knew each other, and there was a fondness in their eyes.

"You look a sight," said Mrs. Tower, appearing amused at the way the old woman was dressed. "I hardly knew you till you came up close."

Addie was further surprised when her grandmother laughed.

"It's only to fool people like those ladies who just came around," said Addie. She knew her grandmother was uncomfortable in Emmaline's dresses, and she wished they didn't need such a subterfuge.

"I saw those lady visitors," said Nokummus when she got to the stoop, sat on the edge of it, and put down her basket. "What did they want?"

"They wanted to know about you, about why I wasn't in school, but Mrs. Tower set them straight," said Addie. She thought she might as well add the part about school. She'd been wanting to bring it up. "They seemed to be satisfied with what she told them."

"And what did you tell them, Mrs. Tower?"

"The truth," said Mrs. Tower. Addie thought how she had been ashamed for some time that she hadn't always told it in the past. "I told her that you're Addie's real grandmother, and that she'll soon be going back to school."

"School?" Nokummus questioned, but Mrs. Tower had stated it as if it were a fact, and Addie could have hugged her for it.

# *thirty-five*

NOKUMMUS MOVED ABOUT THE HOUSE all day as stealthily as Matilda. It was clear the coming of those women had disturbed her.

When John arrived later, he coaxed Addie out-of-doors, and they walked in the fields. He wasn't as talkative as usual, and his guarded words when he did speak made Addie uneasy. He seemed to be beating around the bush, and it wasn't until she asked him a direct question that he opened up.

"What's this all about?"

"It's about what you told me. What you said was the truth of things. Ma sent me to see Dr. Perkins, and he backed you up. She said she knowed about it from the start. And there were others suspected as much."

"Others like Clive's mother?"

"Her and others."

"You act as if I have some awful disease or something, as if those people, whoever they are, think I have it, too."

"It's just—just such a peculiar piece of news. Like everything I thought I knew for sure been turned on its head."

"I'm still the same."

He looked at her intently for so long that Addie had to look away. And then he said, "You are. It took a while to figure out. But you are." He continued to search her face. "Though a darn sight more sure of yourself. You don't ask so many questions anymore."

She smiled up at him in a shy way that made her wonder at such a rush of timid feelings.

There were tiny wrinkles forming at the corners of his mouth, as if he wanted to smile, too, but didn't know if he should. Then his demeanor became so serious so suddenly that Addie was confused.

"So if I'm still the same, and you believe the things I've told you, why are you scowling?"

He took off his cap and held it in both hands. The breeze picked up the tips of his hair and riffled the shocks as if they were a deck of cards. Addie looked at his face, a boy's face, not yet a man, and she thought of the way he took charge of things, of how he made decisions for himself. She hoped she was becoming like him in some of those ways.

He cleared his throat, put his cap back on his head, and reached for her hand. It was a natural gesture, she supposed, friend to friend, but he'd never done it before. She was aware again of how large his hands had become, and she loved how he held her small one with such gentle strength. When his arm went around her waist, she wanted it to stay there forever. Was this how White Moon had felt, she wondered, when Addie's father had held her?

"I keep thinking how you're gonna want to leave," he said, "to go back with Nokummus. It's clear as day now that the old woman's been hanging around these parts for years, just so as she could one day bring you back to wherever it is she came from."

"Doesn't mean I have to go with her." Right now the thought of being so far away from John seemed incomprehensible. But what if the old woman was right, and her father never returned? Addie realized with new clarity that in such a case, Nokummus would be all the family she had left.

"She's got her ways," John said, and Addie knew exactly what he meant. She'd been afraid that no matter what she did or said, no matter how she stuck to her guns, her grandmother would somehow work her magic and get what she wanted.

"But she has to wait until Pa comes home," Addie said, dismissing her fears about her pa's well-being. "When he comes home, she'll see that I belong here with him." *And with you,* she thought with a new conviction.

"Don't be too sure. And don't be countin' on his coming anytime soon. The fellas at the yards say that even if the ones who had been on the *Metropolis* take the shorter route back through Central America, it'll take 'em two months at least to get here."

Knowing how much longer it had taken for Pa's ship to go around Cape Horn, Addie was surprised it could actually take only two months for the men to get back to Massachusetts, and she was giddy with the thought of it. There was so much she wanted to tell her father. So much about their life here that was completely changed. And she needed to know just why it was that Pa hadn't taken better care of her grandmother. She needed him to apologize to Nokummus. If Addie was ever to forgive him, he had to do that.

"Here," Addie said to John as she took his father's watch from her pocket and put it in his hand. "I've been meaning to give this back." For all the weeks on the island, she hadn't had a need to know the time, and the watch was no longer wound.

He turned it over. "Didn't you use it?" he asked.

"When I was in the shipyard, it helped keep track of the days. I needed it real badly then."

He pressed it back into her palm. "Then keep it for a time when you may need it again."

"But it's your pa's."

"He's got another now. It's got a bigger face that's easier to read. Besides, I want to give you something you can keep for good and all. Something that makes you think of me from time to time."

How could she not think of John! She thought of him more and more with every day. "Thank you," she said, that same shyness returning to confound her.

John had also brought live chickens this time and set them in the empty henhouse. Though not the ones Addie had given him, he claimed they were good layers just the same. She looked forward to the taste of fresh eggs again, and as soon as he left, she went back to the house to tell Nokummus.

The old woman was sitting cross-legged once more before the unlit fire, the back of each hand resting on a knee. Her eyes were closed, and she chanted a string of words in Wampanoag, using the low songlike voice Addie had heard many times before. Though a swath of sunlight fell across her through the gaping door, Nokummus didn't open her eyes or interrupt her reverie. The girl stood above her for several minutes, studying the loosened bush of coarse white hair that framed her wrinkled face and the collection of deerskin clothing she had put on again.

Except for the finite movement of her lips, her figure seemed frozen in place, even as the shadows of late afternoon began to shrink the rooms and pull a train of stillness through them, one by one.

Hesitant to interrupt this long meditation, Addie prepared a simple supper of fried onions, potatoes, and dried haddock, hoping the cooking odors would rouse her grandmother. When this approach didn't seem to be working, the girl called her gently and set a place for them both at the table.

For a short while, the singing chant continued, but then Nokummus gave a long sigh and rose as if she'd been asleep. When she did come to the table, she seemed not altogether present and didn't look up from the food that she picked at with disinterest.

"When the white ladies come again," she suddenly blurted out, "we will not pretend. We will not show such shame for our ancestors."

It had seemed necessary to Addie that they pretend. What she wanted was to be left alone until her father came home, which, she realized now, might be sooner than she'd first thought. When the townspeople recognized Nokummus as the old Indian woman who lived off the land from season to season, Addie was afraid they'd intervene in some way. She needed to keep them away for the short time until Pa returned. She needed to attend school again to show that she was cared for and well, and then none of those folks from the town would get the notion to interfere.

She tried to explain this and the fact that summer vacation was coming soon, and she would just be away from Nokummus for a short time during the days until then. But Addie's grandmother seemed to view such behavior as a final step that would separate them and bind Addie to this town of shipbuilders. Addie had to remind herself that a shipbuilder had, after all, stolen her grandmother's daughter.

But when Nokummus told her again that she was needed as *pauwau* of the tribe, Addie stood up to her grandmother in a more forceful way than ever before. By now she'd had time to put all the pieces of the puzzling dream in place, and she felt certain of what she was about to declare. Still, she knew it would be upsetting to the old woman to have to consider things as Addie saw them, and she chose her words carefully.

"Remember how Hobbamock didn't have a meeting with me during my vision quest? Remember how you said he would, but then he didn't?"

"Perhaps you did not recognize him."

"Not recognize the Warrior Spirit!"

"It is possible."

"It's also possible that he didn't want to meet with me for other reasons."

"Foolish talk."

"I have thought about this for a long time, Grandmother. And the answer is very clear to me."

Nokummus looked hard at Addie. Her dark eyes jumped about as if she was astounded at the effrontery of her grand-daughter and afraid of what the girl was about to reveal. Addie put her hand on the woman's shoulder to steady her. It felt knobby and frail in her grasp, and she regretted the need to tell Nokummus what she firmly believed to be true.

"Just as the white people don't want a half-breed in their midst, doesn't it make sense that the Wampanoag people might have similar feelings about those of mixed blood? Why would they want to elevate me, no matter what promise you say I have shown, to the high office of *pauwau*? Hobbamock knows that there is no pact he can make with me."

Nokummus did not seem surprised, but she did put a hand to her head as if consulting with her inner self, and when she finally glanced over at Addie, her eyes held a help-less look like that of a child pleading with a parent. *She had suspected this*, thought Addie. *The old woman had suspected what I just told her, but she had refused to accept it.*

Nokummus's utter silence confirmed all of Addie's suppo-sitions and broke her heart.

# *thirty-six*

IN THE DAYS AHEAD, Addie would take the long walk to school each morning and return home just before dark to care for the animals. Sometimes John went with her, but often he'd have work in the yards. And Nokummus would frequently be off somewhere in the early morning hours and not in the house at nightfall. Addie wondered if it was a way of punishing her for what she had said and for her decision to return to school, a decision of which the old woman steadfastly disapproved.

In the classroom, Addie had been welcomed back by most of the children, especially the youngest ones, who looked up to her. She was relieved to hear that Clive was out for the hay making and probably wouldn't be back to finish the year. Fanny Bright had moved to a desk at the other side of the room and barely glanced at Addie. "You look different," she said as they passed on the way to the privy. "Taller or something"—as if that wasn't what she meant at all. Addie's desk was much as it had been, her inkwell nearly full, her copybook almost blank. She had started a new one just before she'd run away. One of the Lucy books she'd been reading to the younger girls, *Lucy at the Seashore*, still held her bookmark. And there was a November copy of *Youth's Penny Gazette* that she realized she'd never even opened. She remembered how Miss Fitzgibbon had saved that issue especially for her.

"The book on the China trade was burned," she told Miss Fitzgibbon at the earliest opportunity. It had been a beautiful book with lovely pictures.

"I heard there had been . . . an unfortunate fire," said Miss Fitzgibbon, and Fanny snickered. "But we're through with the China trade for now," added the teacher as she handed Addie another more familiar book. "We're finishing up this edition, dear. See what you can do to catch up."

Addie felt no pleasure in returning to her McGuffey Reader, and when she came upon an essay on American Indians in which they were referred to as *savages*, she winced both at the word as it applied to her and to the fact that only a few months ago she wouldn't have noticed such a slur.

The building of a high school had recently been approved by the school board, and Miss Fitzgibbon was as excited about the possibilities as if she were one of the students headed there. On the blackboard she wrote the names of the subjects they hoped to include in the curriculum. Natural history and grammar were familiar enough topics, but Addie had never heard of mineralogy or zoology or drawing with perspective or languages such as Latin. It would be months until the building was finished, but just knowing there would soon be such a place, a place to learn any number of practical and exotic things, put a lump in her throat and filled her with a shimmery dismay at all the possibilities in this world of which she hadn't even been aware.

Earlier in the week, Miss Fitzgibbon had loaned John a book called *An Arithmetical and Commercial Dictionary.*

"This'll be bound to help you in your trade, don't you know," she'd said, "even if your choice is not to go on to the high school." And even if their lives, hers and John's, would not always be exactly in step, it didn't lessen Addie's amazement at these wonderful ideas and books that seemed to be coming from nowhere and yet must have been there all along. And she knew that John, no matter what he decided to do, would still be in Essex and still nearby.

As she came close to home in the late afternoon, she noticed that Fleur had been put out to pasture. It was usually something that Addie took care of when she returned from school. Still full of the news about the high school and needing to tell someone, she searched inside and outside the house for her grandmother, even though she felt certain the old woman would not want to hear what she had to say. Not finding her in either place, she went out to the barn, rested her head against the neck of Little Star, and whispered all her pent-up information. When the horse whinnied at the sound of her voice, she threw a saddle onto her back and rode her out into the fields. Though not strictly in search of Nokummus, Addie looked deep into the wooded areas and scanned the distance for any sign of a moving figure.

It wasn't until the red sun began to burnish the land with crimson light that she turned the horse toward home. She'd brought Fleur into the barn for the night and rubbed down Little Star before she started up the path. From there she could see someone standing tall in the open doorway. The figure was framed in candlelight and displayed a kind of determination she could sense even from this distance. On coming closer, she recognized Nokummus, who was dressed in the clothes she had worn when living in the wild and was standing as straight as a tree while resting on a birch limb that had been fashioned into a walking stick.

"It is time for me to go," said the old woman when Addie came close. "To be with my people."

"To go? When? Surely not tonight?"

"I will leave at the first light of morning," said Nokummus, "as is proper for any Wampanoag."

Addie took her grandmother's arm and led her back into the front room. "But your tribe is so far away. How will you get there?"

"I will get there in the same way that I came. I will walk."

She had never told Addie before how she'd made the trip to find her daughter, and the girl was astounded.

"I took a boat from the island when I came to the mainland, and then I walked."

"But that was a long time ago," said Addie. Her own lifetime ago. "You were stronger then."

"Yes," said Nokummus. She did not dispute the truth of what Addie said. "But it is time. I cannot stay. I can no longer live in this house. You say your father will be home soon. If that is true, you will not need me, and I will have to go."

Addie had known she was uncomfortable here. The old woman had never tried to hide it. But the girl had hoped these feelings were only temporary.

"I'll need you more than ever," cried Addie. "Papa and I will both need you. And it's warm here. It's dry. We have enough food. And now we even have eggs and milk."

"But there are ghosts. Ghosts of the white lady. Ghosts of her child. Things belonging to the man who robbed me of my daughter."

Addie felt no presence of ghosts. Only memories. Happy memories. How she wished there were a small Jack ghost around the house for even a little while or the ghost of Mama saying, "Run out and play, Adelaide. Enjoy the sunshine." But still she realized, had realized from the start, how foreign the things here must seem to Nokummus.

"Please," she pleaded. "Don't leave until Papa comes home. Papa can take you back to your island by ship."

"Papa! What makes Papa so important? Why is his house better than my house? Why is his money better than mine?" She flung a wad of paper bills onto the table.

"Where did you get those?" asked Addie.

"Emerson Hayden gave them often. What use are they to me? I usually threw them in the river."

So Papa had tried to take care of her. But why hadn't he provided a roof over her head?

"This house is like the other house after you were born. There is no smell of the forest. Little sound of birds."

"Did you live in that other house with my father?"

"I took care of you until he found a woman to marry. After that I built my own *wetu*. I would not go when the white lady came for me."

So Mama had tried to take her in, too. It must have been a huge step for Emmaline, as sensitive as she was to the judgment of the townspeople. And for Papa, who clearly had wanted to save Addie from the stigma of her mixed blood. She was just beginning to understand about that, but she still resented having been left ignorant of her heritage for so long.

She sensed that this was no time to berate the old woman for her grudges and fierce independence. But what she absolutely had to do was keep Nokummus from leaving. The aged woman would probably die on a long trip on foot such as she had described. Addie had only until the first light of morning to think of a plan to keep her grandmother from harm.

# *thirty-seven*

WHEN ADDIE CLIMBED TO HER TRUNDLE in the loft, Nokummus was fully clothed and sitting upright in a straight-back chair as if she planned to take off at any moment. By lying with her own head at the foot of the bed, the girl discovered that she could see enough of her grandmother to notice any movement. Candles had been snuffed out, and there was only light from a gibbous moon outlining the still figure of the woman. Determined not to doze off while the old one looked poised to escape, Addie did arithmetic tables in her head and added sums. She thought of all the stories she would soon be telling her father, of how distraught he would be when he discovered that Emmaline and Jack were gone. After the shock of it, and in spite of the grief he was bound to feel, she hoped he would be proud of her resourcefulness. She imagined his praise, the way he would hold her away from him and look at her with admiration. He'd tell her how pleased he was with the decisions she had made and all that she had learned.

As her eyelids grew heavy, she made a tent of her fingers and watched the supple formations she could create by simply folding them together and stretching them apart. She walked them up and down her bent knees and across the coverlet. Once she slid from under the covers and over to the stairs, where she could get a fuller view of Nokummus. The old woman's head had fallen forward and was resting on her chest; she was sound asleep, even though her body continued to stay upright. Heavy breathing broken by tiny snorts and whistles proved it. It seemed pointless to keep watch after that. The old woman would sleep like this until morning, and Addie could no longer keep her own eyes open.

It was still dark when she bolted from her bed with an acute awareness of the early hour and the sense that light would soon begin to sift through the rooms, even though objects continued to be indistinct. She crept down the stairs, hoping not to wake Nokummus. When she padded quietly to the chair, however, it was empty.

Her grandmother had said she would leave at first light. Because she had always kept her word, Addie thought she might just be out at the privy, but then she noticed that her satchel and baskets were gone as well. And the walking stick! The walking stick was no longer resting against the wall. Addie sank into the chair herself and tried to think of what to do. She knew the direction Nokummus would take, but not how long she'd been gone. In the past, when Addie had thought of her as nothing more than a peddler, the old woman had been clever at hiding in and around the town. She had sometimes disappeared for weeks and would turn up only when it seemed to suit her. But that was before there had been any bond between the two, before Addie had known that the same blood ran in their veins, before having a grandmother — this grandmother — had mattered so much.

She dressed in the breeches and cap she wore when riding Little Star, secured Matilda in the house, and went into the barn to rouse the horse. So often she wished she could speak her language so she could explain to her beloved pet all the comings and goings of the people the animal had become accustomed to, and those that, sadly, had sometimes left her behind. The weather had been mild for some time now, but this morning the air was heavy with moisture that filtered very slowly from a low layer of clouds. Only the faint aura of the yellow sun could be seen in the east. When she rode out into the fields and pastureland, thin streaks of light slashed the dark sky. Nokummus would need to travel around the edges of the town, skirting the shipyards and the causeway, and so Addie took Little Star even farther than Bullock's field, searching for any shadowy movement. A deer bounded across her path on its way from the river; the eyes of a fox glistened in the dark woods. Even if Nokummus had left hours ago, Addie reasoned, she would not have been able to cover more ground than this.

Reluctantly, she turned the horse around and guided her in slowly retracing her steps. Though still overcast, the day had brightened enough so Addie could see into small pockets of the forest and for miles into the empty distance. Where had her grandmother gone? She had disappeared so completely, and yet Addie could not imagine her being able to walk for the time it would take to travel even a few miles in the dark. Not knowing where to look next, she took Little Star back to the barn and went into the house for warmer, drier clothing and to collect her thoughts.

When she opened the door, she saw immediately that the chair was occupied once again and that Nokummus was the one sitting in it, wide awake.

"Where have you been?" asked Addie. "Where did you go?"

"Not far," said Nokummus. "You cannot make a journey in the rain."

This was news to Addie. They had moved about before with no thought to such things. But she was grateful that, whatever the reason, her grandmother was here in front of her and not hurt or lost somewhere in the wilderness. Still she couldn't help herself from saying, "It isn't really raining yet. It's just a drizzle."

"There is another reason," the old woman said. She kneaded her hands together and seemed to be struggling with what was to come next. When she did speak, her voice quavered with uncharacteristic emotion.

"The other reason is that you may be wrong to expect your father to return. If he does fail to come back, you will be alone. All alone. You would be all alone all over again."

Addie had been so concerned for her grandmother that she hadn't even stopped to consider that part. Yes, she would be alone again, but she knew now that she could handle that. What she couldn't handle was the loss of this person almost as dear to her as her own pa. Knowing that Nokummus would be uncomfortable in an embrace, Addie simply smiled, wrapped her grandmother carefully in a blanket, and brought her some hot sassafras tea. Matilda rubbed against Nokummus's leg and purred, something she hadn't done since her mysterious trip back from the island.

John came by later in the day with news of the returning men of the *Metropolis*. Second mate John Quiner and third mate Mr. Fisher had traveled the Panama route and were already back in Essex. Addie's father had indeed chosen to go through Central America as John had guessed, but he was well on his way. No one in the Essex County and California Mining and Trading Company had struck it rich.

The last part didn't seem to register with Addie.

"Didn't you hear what I said, Addie?" asked John. "They've all lost every last penny of what they invested. There won't be any gold for sure."

Addie thought of her quahog shell, the wampum Nokummus had told her about. She could feel the smooth lining of it in her hand, could see the gradations in color from dark purple to blue to shiny white. How could gold be more valuable than that? She thought of how when Pa got back, they would make a life again and one day he could take Nokummus safely home to her people. Addie would go, too, and stay long enough to learn about her ancestral lands and meet her relatives and make sure her grandmother was settled again within the tribe.

Addie knew that she was bound to lose Nokummus sometime, but it wouldn't be today. She would ask the Great Father and, of course, Spider Grandmother, to make certain that it wouldn't be for at least another season of fiddleheads, at least one more Grass Moon.

IN THE GOLD of summer
he sprints through fields

like a returning warrior,
arms outstretched,

and I call "Papa"
as I reach for him

and ask the question that I've held inside
so long: "Why did you lie to me

about my mother? Why?"
He takes my face between his hands,

an answer forming in his eyes. His voice
is broken when he says, "I wanted to protect you."

His face is wet, as if he has been told
what happened here.

He says the names — *my Emmaline, my Jack* —
and bends to me and weeps into my hair.

To share a grief I've carried
by myself these many months

is staggering and strange. And yet
there is relief in it

and a feeling that I've felt before
but do not recognize right then,

not right away. It is a while
before I know to call it trust.

    •    •    •

ACKNOWLEDGMENTS

There are a number of people I'd like to thank for their generous help with this book. They include Laurie Jacobs, Chris Brodien Jones, Donna McArdle, and Patricia Bridgeman, all of whom read chapters from the manuscript in progress and gave invaluable suggestions. I'm grateful as well for the expertise of Ellen Wittlinger and Nancy Werlin, who helped to hone the work when it was near completion, and I deeply appreciate the expert counsel of Annawon Weeden, Wampanoag teacher and storyteller. Lastly, thanks are certainly due to my meticulous editor, Hilary Van Dusen, who continues to save me from the small and large errors that can undermine a book, and to my agent, Lauren Abramo, for her efforts on my behalf and her sage advice.

The resources for this book are too numerous to mention here, but the most valuable ones were *The Argonauts of '49: History and Adventures of the Emigrant Companies from Massachusetts, 1849–1850* by Octavius Thorndike Howe, *Empowerment of North American Indian Girls* by Carol A. Markstrom, and *The Shipbuilders of Essex* by Dana A. Story. The Beverly Historical Society and the Essex Shipbuilding Museum were helpful sources as well.